Spirits in Savannah

A Doctor Danger Mystery

HEATHER SILVIO

Panther Books

Panther Books: Tampa, FL & Portland, OR.

Visit the author's website at https://www.heathersilvio.com
Contact the author at: heather@heathersilvio.com

Cover design by Sonia Freitas at Chloe Belle Arts
https://www.ChloeBelleArts.com

Library of Congress Control Number: 2023912318
ISBN (Print) 978-1-951192-24-2
ISBN (E-book) 978-1-951192-21-1

BOOKS BY HEATHER SILVIO

DOCTOR DANGER MYSTERIES

Hazard in Hawaii (#1)

PARANORMAL TALENT AGENCY

Lights, Camera, Action (Episode One)

Reset to One (Episode Two)

That's a Wrap (Episode Three)

An Unexpected Sequel (Episode Four)

Jumping the Shark (Episode Five)

The Season Finale (Episode Six)

Paranormal Talent Agency Episodes 1-3 Collection

Paranormal Talent Agency Episodes 4-6 Collection

Paranormal Talent Agency Episodes 1-6 Collection

NON-SERIES FICTION

Not Quite Famous

Beyond the Abyss

Courting Death

NONFICTION

Special Snowflake Syndrome

Happiness by the Numbers

Stress Disorders: A Healing Path for PTSD

CHAPTER ONE

That I wanted to rip someone's head off within five minutes of meeting the family confirmed they needed supernatural help.

"Sarah, are you okay?" Daniel Trawl, my part-time assistant, asked, worry clouding his hazel eyes.

Christine Mackey, our client, looked from Dan to me. "Dr. Danger?"

"Give me a second, please," I managed to answer. As a clairempath, I experienced others' emotions as if they were my own. The seething anger coursing through me wasn't mine.

I identified and isolated the anger, breathing slowly to calm the accompanying nervous system overreaction, and surrounded the emotion with a bubble. As I exhaled, I imagined the bubble floating away, taking the anger with it. My breathing slowed and my heart rate stopped jumping around. The urge to beat someone to a bloody pulp passed with the anger. Eyes closed, I imagined my medieval stone wall, the image that provided protection from others' invading emotions. The wall grew higher as I placed gray stones upon moss-covered stones, piling them toward the sky in my mind. When I felt better fortified, I opened my eyes and offered a wide smile to the Mackey family, staring at me askance.

"Are you okay?" Christine echoed Dan's question.

"I am now, yes," I assured them, not elaborating. "How are you all doing?" The Mackeys had hired me to investigate what they believed was a supernatural issue. It was a specialty that I'd fallen into as a private investigator's assistant while earning my master's degree in counseling. My boss, Jeffrey McCarthy, shocked me by gifting me the business when his retirement coincided with my second graduation a few years later, when I received my doctorate in comparative mythology.

Although the blog Dan wrote about our supernatural exploits blew the whole thing up. *A Doctor Danger Mystery* had become a mini-phenomenon. Now I ran my firm as a Supernatural Specialist, while teaching occasional classes at a Tampa community college. Dan accompanied me on our out-of-town cases. The final member of our ragtag team, Amanda Jenkins, stayed in Tampa to do research as needed.

Right now, Dan and I sat on a cloth-covered couch at the crack of dawn in a Savannah, Georgia vacation rental.

The family sitting across from us looked like they hadn't slept in weeks. Which it turned out they hadn't.

"As we explained when we hired you, we're desperate," Christine began, her hands fidgeting in her lap. She glanced at her husband and their two teenagers. All four had huge bags under their brown, blood-shot eyes.

Christine's long, curly brown hair was pulled back in a messy ponytail. Her husband, James, had what appeared to be at least a week's worth of uneven facial hair growth. He kept running his hand over it, which made me think the beard wasn't usual for him. He slumped forward on the couch, his elbows on his knees.

Fifteen-year-old Kelsey let her long, curly brown hair fall so that it obscured part of her face. She had wrapped her arms so tightly around her thin middle that I worried she'd asphyxiate herself. And, 18-year-old Jimmy stared at the ground, a frown slashing his pimply face, long arms and legs suggesting a gangly teen undergoing perhaps his final growth spurt.

"Of course," I said, recognizing that calling a supernatural investigative consultant was not a typical call for most people.

"We wanted to meet with you here because this is where we think everything began," she said in a soft voice.

My angry reaction upon entering the vacation rental suggested something was going on in this house, but I wasn't sure yet what that was. "Here specifically, or Savannah more generally?"

James jumped in to answer before his wife. "We've

thought about that a lot in the past two weeks. It started with the ghost tour we took during our vacation."

The Mackeys had told me earlier that they'd traveled from their home in Tennessee to Savannah for a final ten-day vacation before their son left for college in California. They'd filled their days with a variety of tours; everything from a self-guided walking tour of the town's famous squares to a group foodie tour to the nighttime ghost tour that seemed to start the trouble.

"We didn't realize it at first," Christine picked up the narrative. "But, all four of us realized over the next two days that we'd had dreams of pirates."

At the word pirates, a frisson of anger rolled through me. Interesting, and not good. I rolled my shoulders and added a stone to my medieval wall of protection. Something or someone was triggered by the word.

She tittered. "We assumed it was because of the pirate history of Savannah that we'd learned about."

"What kind of pirate dreams were these?" Perhaps I could narrow in on why the word created that reaction. The teenagers stared at me. Both looked scared, with a touch of insolence. I barely managed not to laugh out loud. Teenagers. That likely had nothing to do with the case and everything to do with hormones and lack of sleep.

Christine and James exchanged an unhappy glance and James answered. "Weird, to be honest. We talked about it once we realized we were all having similar dreams. The dreams jumped around, like dreams do. Some scenes took place on what looked like pirate ships."

"The images were like what we'd seen in the pirate museum," Christine added.

"Other scenes took place on a beach, like at a camp out." James shrugged, appearing unsure how to better describe the dreams.

"The last scenes took place at a bar or restaurant filled with drunks and pirates, all dressed in old-timey clothing." Christine bounced her leg until her husband laid a hand on her knee. She covered his hand with her own and sighed. "That would have been fine, but then the hallucinations…" Her words trailed off.

"When did the hallucinations begin?" I asked, noting that Dan was using a stylus to scribble everything they said into our growing case document opened on his tablet.

"Almost immediately after arriving home," Christine answered, her face paling even more if that was possible.

"We started seeing pirates walking around our house," James said. "I know that sounds ridiculous."

"It doesn't," I said gently. "Tell me more about what you saw." Another ripple of anger wormed through me and my jaw clenched. The protective wall normally worked better than this. A lot of angry energy existed in this room. Except none of the family looked that angry. The son still scowled, but I couldn't tell if the emotion was originating from him.

"Jimmy, Kelsey," I said, surprising the teens by addressing them. "Why don't you tell me what you've seen at your home?"

The teenagers exchanged a look, much as their parents

had, and Kelsey swallowed audibly. "Just what Dad said," she answered with a one-shoulder shrug.

"Yeah," Jimmy agreed, staring over my shoulder at something apparently very fascinating.

"What are you looking at that has you so mesmerized?" I asked, and Jimmy's hard gaze swung to mine. Was that normal teenage defiance, or something more?

"Nothing," he murmured, dropping his gaze and slouching against the arm of the couch.

I redirected my questions to his parents; I'd have to circle back around to the teenagers less directly. "It worsened when you were home, but you wanted to meet here because the dreams started here," I summarized and gestured at the room around us. It was a lovely vacation rental. I could see why it would be popular. Gleaming hardwood floors, and a soaring ceiling above large windows that flooded the room with sunlight. The furniture was serviceable; maybe a little older, but comfortable enough, with a pleasant country-chic style that would stand up to consistent use.

Christine nodded. "Yes, precisely. We thought maybe it would be helpful to walk the tour and see if something jumped out at us."

"But it didn't?" I asked.

The corners of her mouth drooped. "No."

James stared at me in defeat. "We didn't know what else to do. Then we saw Dan's blog when we were searching for answers online. So we called you."

"Thank you so much for meeting us on such short notice, and so early." Christine wrapped an arm around her daughter's frame. "We haven't gotten a good night's sleep in weeks. And we're jumping out of our skin, waiting for the next hallucination. Nothing like this has ever happened before."

"No history of supernatural issues?" I asked.

"Nothing," Christine answered.

"Even something simple, like knowing who's calling without checking caller ID? Or seeing, hearing, even smelling something that doesn't seem to have a source? Anything that, looking back, you can't fully explain?"

"Nothing like that," Christine said. The other family members shook their heads as well.

"Do you think you can help us?" Jimmy blurted out.

"I don't know," I admitted. "But I'm going to try."

"Do you think we've been supernaturally infected or something?" Kelsey asked, her brother's question emboldening her.

I shook my head. "Any number of things could be going on. Savannah has an incredibly rich and diverse history, not all of it pleasant. It's certainly possible that there's a supernatural component to what's happening. Or it could be a shared psychosis," I said, trying and failing to lighten the mood with a joke. Dan made a choking sound, and I resisted the urge to look at him. He got the joke, but if I saw him laughing, I'd compound the damage.

"You think we're psychotic?" Christine asked, her expression aghast.

Ugh. Macabre humor had been a mistake. I hurried to explain. "Sorry, bad psychology joke. No, I don't believe you have psychosis."

"Then what?" Jimmy demanded, tension radiating off of him.

"I don't know, but I'll do my best to find out." A wave of malevolent glee swept through me. "If I care to," slipped out before I caught myself. Five pairs of eyes widened, though Dan immediately understood something emotional had happened to me.

"Sarah, do you need another minute?" he asked, his hand at my elbow.

The physical touch electrified me instead of grounding me. I leaped to my feet, then strode to the doorway arch to the bedroom, behind the couch where the family sat.

Dan stood but did not follow, while the family twisted in their seats to watch me.

I added yet another stone to my not-so-effective medieval wall. At this rate, it would reach the heavens. "Apologies," I said, voice shaky to my ears. But before I could lay out my plan, my vision wavered as I fought off another wave of that weird, happy anger. "Oh my goodness."

Next to the window closest to the couch on which the family perched now stood a young man. Scraggly long black hair surrounded a youthful face. He wore a white shirt with puffy sleeves, open at the throat, over black pants and black scuffed boots. He had a pistol strapped to one hip and a knife in a sheath on the other.

A pirate! And he stared at me with insane blue eyes.

"Oh good," he said jauntily. "Ye can see me. That will make this much more fun."

CHAPTER TWO

"Who are you?" I asked the pirate, eliciting gasps and a flurry of questions from the family watching me from the couch. If Dan responded to my question, I didn't hear him.

"Who do you see?"

"Is it a pirate?"

"Does this mean we're not hallucinating?"

"Are our visions real?"

The questions overlapped so much that I failed to discern who asked each one. Not that it mattered. I only had eyes for the man who had blinked into visual existence.

The pirate by the window sneered. "Why should I tell ye?"

"Who are you?" My repeated question now dripped with restrained anger.

The pirate's sneer became a smile, revealing rotting, snaggled teeth. "'Tis different." He stepped toward me, his ghost boots silent on the hardwood floors.

"What?" I asked, even though I knew the answer, as his wonder at my matching anger mingled with that anger in my mind.

"Ho, ho, ho." The pirate slapped his thigh.

"Heh, heh, heh," I echoed his laughter. He was right. The whole situation was highly entertaining. A ghost? Of a pirate? In Savannah? I mean, what could be more perfect?

"Sarah."

Dan's tone caught my attention more than my name. The mischievous glee stampeding through me belonged to the ghost. Ugh. Normally I caught on faster to the invading emotions of others.

The ghost seemed off, to be sure, but I tried for civil and approachable, anyway. "My name is Sarah Danger. I'm a specialist who—"

"I care why?" The ghost leaned against the back of the couch I'd been sitting on before his appearance. I always wondered how an intangible ghost could lean against a physical object on another plane; somehow they chose to lean against things as if they had corporeal form. That allowed them to 'walk' on the ground, too.

The fact that all four family members and Dan also now stood from the couches watching me talk to the air registered in my peripheral vision.

"If you don't want to give me your name, can you tell me why you're here?" I asked instead of answering, hoping I'd get lucky.

No such luck. The unnamed pirate ghost laughed again. "Why are ye here?" he asked the question of me, oblivious to the fact he had just cut me off when I'd tried to provide that information moments before.

"The Mackeys hired me to free them of the pirate ghost who has been haunting them." I said the sentence as neutrally as possible, my goal to perhaps elicit a real response but without another angry flare.

"'Tis funny coming from them," the pirate retorted, his face scrunched and his hands fisted.

"What do you—"

The pirate ghost vanished.

"Wait!" I cried out, but the ghost was indeed gone.

My cry alerted the Mackeys to the probable departure of whatever being I'd been conversing with. Questions inundated me from the haunted family.

"You saw him?" Christine asked.

"Was it a pirate?" Kelsey asked.

"Can you describe who or what you saw?" James asked.

"Oh, goody, you've got our psychosis," Jimmy quipped, throwing my words back in my face.

"Sarah, are you okay?" Dan's question enabled me to focus on him as the last of the ghost's malevolent glee drained away.

I held up a hand to stop the barrage of questions and comments. "I can confirm that there is a pirate ghost present in this home."

The family clutched at each other, jaws dropped open and eyes wide at me confirming their fears.

"I suspect he is indeed haunting you," I continued.

"Just suspect?" James frowned.

"That isn't something I can say with complete certainty. Given his comments," I added, then faltered with how much to disclose. The ghost had indicated the family knew something I didn't. Without understanding the scope of the haunting, the ghost's exact verbiage could hold importance I didn't yet comprehend. And I didn't want to enlighten the family until I understood that connection. I started my sentence over. "I believe the pirate ghost is haunting your family, yes."

Christine's eyes closed, and she pulled her daughter closer.

"Now what?" James asked.

"The next steps are to confirm the ghost is haunting the family, and how. The ghost can be attached to one of you, all of you, or even an object in your possession." I met Dan's eyes, and he nodded. "One or more of you may have seen, heard, or otherwise experienced something related to your initial visit that resulted in the haunting."

"But we already retraced our steps," Christine said.

"Yes, and you did so together, correct?" Dan jumped in to ask.

"Of course. We wanted to help each other remember what had happened," James answered for the family.

"Dr. Danger is going to interview each of you separately," Dan explained. "She'll ask you to bring her through the timeline to the best of your recollection." Now he held up his hand to stop Christine from interrupting. "She doesn't expect it to be perfect. But, as she noted, one of you may have seen or heard or experienced something different from the others."

"Of course," James said, nodding in understanding. "Not having others there to fill in the blanks of their own experiences could allow one of us to remember something we didn't remember before."

"Exactly," I said, retaking the narrative. "Dan and I are going to head into the bedroom now—" My cheeks heated at the unintended double entendre and I avoided looking in Dan's direction. "—to discuss our planned questions, and then bring each of you in individually." I made eye contact with each of the four family members. "Do any of you have questions before we get started?" A series of head shakes met my question.

What I withheld from the family, and what Dan knew from our history together, was that if the ghost was haunting the family and not the vacation rental, which seemed likely, the ghost almost certainly wasn't haunting the family as a whole, but one of its members. The true next step was determining which family member was the target. And why.

CHAPTER THREE

Dan followed me through the arched doorway from the living room to the primary bedroom of the vacation rental. It was a gorgeous space, similar to the living room, with its vaulted ceiling and large windows along one wall, letting in a ton of light. A massive king-sized bed sat against the wall perpendicular. A loveseat and two high-backed plush chairs pushed against the wall opposite the windows completed the space. I strode toward the loveseat and chairs.

"Perfect. Help me move them?" I asked Dan as I grabbed one chair and turned it to face the loveseat. He repeated the process with the other chair, resulting in an intimate interview setup.

"How do you propose we figure out which family member the ghost is haunting?" Dan asked the question I'd been thinking.

"I'll take them through their timelines, as we stated, but, of course, I'm hoping their emotional energy lets me know which one it is."

"That would make it easier."

He and I shared an easy smile. Ever since our first out-of-town case together to Hawaii, we'd developed an amiable, but platonic, friendship and working relationship. He was my junior by several years, and pursuing his own doctorate to match mine. He enjoyed flirting with me and I enjoyed reminding him that we were colleagues.

"Let's start with the mother."

"You got it, boss."

I took a seat in one of the plush chairs, admiring the scrolling loops on the high-back. Either hand-carved or a well-made replica of an antique. Footsteps on the wood flooring alerted me that Dan and Christine had entered the room. I heard a thud as Dan closed the door behind them.

Christine perched uneasily on the edge of the loveseat, facing me. Dan took the chair next to mine and opened his tablet to take notes.

"What can I answer?" Christine's worry was still etched on her face, but her squared shoulders and strong vocal tone told me she planned to cooperate.

None of her emotions breached my stone wall of protection, suggesting she was not the direct target of the haunting. But I'd push her some to see if anything triggered. After easing into it, of course. No reason to alienate a cooperating client!

I offered a gentle smile. "Let's start easy. Talk me

through your vacation timeline. Start with your original arrival in Savannah. I'll ask clarifying questions as you speak, but otherwise, I'll let you tell the story in your own words."

Christine nodded. "We arrived four weeks ago, on a Sunday. We had a mix of activities planned, including a number of tours, like we mentioned."

"Did you also have free time in the schedule?"

"We did. We used that to go deeper into things that interested us from the planned tours."

"Take me through each of those tours."

"All of them?"

"Yes, please. I know you believe that the trouble started with the nighttime ghost tour. And you're probably right," I allowed with a slight nod. "Just in case, however, we need to be thorough."

"Oh, okay." Christine closed her eyes a moment, gathering her thoughts, maybe determining what to include. "The first full day we followed a self-guided walking tour of the town's squares."

"The famous squares designed by James Oglethorpe?" I asked for confirmation on the off chance she was referring to something obscure, but my research during the drive here suggested these were the squares.

"Yes." She launched into a square-by-square description of their walk, with nothing unusual popping out at me. Specifically, my clairempathic abilities registered no emotional change during the recitation. The squares were unlikely to be part of our problem or solution.

"The next tour was a Southern food tour; they even gave us a map of where we visited so we could go back to places we liked."

"Dan, if you'll get a copy of the map later," I said.

"Sure thing, Doc."

"Please take us through that tour," I directed Christine, who described each of the restaurants and even several of the dishes they had. My stomach growled during the scrumptious-sounding bananas foster French toast. "Apologies for that."

Christine laughed, cutting the lingering tension in the room. "Not at all. I highly recommend trying it."

"I've made a note of that," Dan said, merriment evident in his tone.

"Please continue," I said, and she did, wrapping up the story. Once again, nothing stood out as relevant to our case, nor did her emotions change much beyond minor fluctuations. Certainly nothing like what had happened when I first entered the home and when we discussed the pirate ghost.

Christine paled. "The last tour was the nighttime ghost tour."

"The one that seemed to start the trouble," I reiterated.

She nodded and a single tear slipped out.

I leaned forward to pat her knee. "Take your time. We'll get this."

"Thank you," she whispered. With a shuddering breath, she began the tale.

And once again, despite the heightened emotions she experienced in the retelling, I felt nothing unusual. I risked a glance at Dan, who quirked an eyebrow in question. I shook my head in the negative. The ghost didn't appear to be haunting Christine Mackey.

"Did that help?" she asked, interrupting my internal musings.

"Of course," I assured her. It did, by eliminating her as the ghost's target. "Thank you so much for talking us through your experiences."

"Anything I can do to help our family," she said resolutely.

"If you could send James in," I said.

Christine rose from the chair and headed back to the living room. I heard the murmurs as she answered her family's questions. The closed door between the rooms would have prevented our low voices from penetrating. Soon, footsteps entered the space and James Mackey took the seat across from me.

The difference between husband and wife knocked me sideways. His appearance matched his wife—tired, circles under his eyes, pale skin—but the energy differences were stark. He crawled with ghost energy. Or what I assumed was ghost energy, given the circumstances. The energy wasn't threatening my internal protective wall, but it swirled around Dad. I'd tread carefully here, and see what James revealed that might allow me to confirm the ghost was haunting him.

"What do you need to know?" James asked, leaning

forward with hands clasped and elbows resting on his knees. His eyes probed mine, but there was no energy change.

"Your wife talked us through the timeline of your trip from her perspective," I began. "I'd like to hear the same from you. As you noted before, without someone else to fill in gaps, distinct memories may come to the surface."

James nodded, and his lips thinned in thought. "The first tour we took was the walking tour."

"Where did the tour take you?"

He proceeded to tell a story similar to Christine's regarding their walking tour of Savannah's squares. Minor differences existed in the telling, but nothing that human quirks of memory couldn't explain. And his energy level, including the ghost energy, remained steady. It made my skin crawl, but it didn't breach my inner protections.

At my request, James continued through the same timeline that Christine had given, moving from the walking tour to the foodie tour before reaching the nighttime ghost tour.

"That tour was the highlight of the trip," he said, his quiet voice tight with tension.

My heart rate accelerated, and I wanted to flee. Was this anxiety related to the ghost energy I'd felt?

James tapped his sneaker against the hardwood floor.

Mine mimicked his movement, and I swallowed.

"Sarah?" Dan's voice of concern broke through the anxiety flowing from James that had overwhelmed my internal defenses.

"What? What is it?" James asked, his body maintaining its alert readiness, while his head swung between me and Dan.

Dan's use of my name snapped me from my reverie. I isolated the anxiety from James and expelled it while answering his question. "How anxious would you say you are right now, on a scale of 1 to 10, with one being very little, and 10 being the most you've ever had?"

"Huh, what?" James stared at me wide-eyed, then the question sunk in and he coughed. "Ah, right." He took several deep breaths. "Probably a 9, to answer your question. But you just wanted to know if I was aware of being anxious."

His insight surprised me. "Yes. Your anxiety seemed strong," I said, choosing not to add that I wanted to identify if it was coming from him or a ghostly hitchhiker.

"Thinking about the ghost tour, knowing that may have caused all of this." He shook his head. "It freaks me out," he admitted.

As he spoke, he visibly relaxed, but I grew more confused. Perhaps all the anxiety belonged to him. "When you're ready, take me through the ghost tour."

James closed his eyes, much like his wife had done. When he opened them, he launched into another tale that was similar enough to Christine's that it seemed likely to be true. When he finished talking us through the haunted homes and alleyways on the tour, he leaned back, as if a weight had been lifted.

"Feel better?" I asked.

"Yes," James answered. "I don't know if that helped, but knowing I'm giving you everything I can to help my family—" He picked imaginary lint off his jeans. "I'm just glad I could."

"Me too," I said and reached out a hand. He took it and we shared a moment. "Just a few follow-up questions and then we'll talk to the kids." With his consent, I asked my remaining clarifying questions, but I wasn't sure now if he was the one being haunted.

I asked him to step back out into the living room after I asked my last question.

He stood and turned back toward me at the doorway. "Do you want me to send in Jimmy?"

"Not yet. Let me review what you and Christine gave us first," I said.

James left the room, and pulled the door closed behind him.

"What is it?" Dan asked. He scrolled through his interview notes on the tablet. "Did I miss something?"

I jumped up from the chair and paced a tight circle between the bed and the closed door. "No, but I think I am."

"What do you mean?" Dan had stood and now leaned against the back of the chair he'd been sitting in.

"When Dad walked in, I sensed supernatural energy."

"Pirate ghost energy?"

"Maybe? Probably?" I lifted a hand in question. "Regardless of the source, it wasn't strong enough to overcome my protections."

"That's good."

"Generally, yes."

"Not this time?"

"It overcame my wall briefly when we first broached the topic of the ghost tour." I nibbled on my lower lip, ignoring that Dan's eyes followed the movement.

"I figured that was why you asked about the anxiety scale."

"His answer and then the subsequent reduction in anxiety suggested human anxiety. Worry about his family. Nothing supernatural."

"What does that mean?"

"I don't know, to be honest." It pained me to say that. "He's either an expert liar—sociopath level—or he's unaware that he's attached to the ghost." I stilled my manic pacing. "There's another option."

"There is?"

"That the emotion is coming directly from the ghost."

"What do you mean?"

"What we've seen in the past is that the haunted human becomes a conduit for the ghost's energy. In this case, maybe the energy around James is from proximity to the ghost himself, not from functioning as a conduit."

"Is that possible?"

"Sure. Why not?" I answered, a bit flippantly, but truthfully.

"So James could be haunted by the ghost. The family's experiences are from the ghost. But they aren't being transmitted through any of them. Am I getting that right?"

"It's a theory."

"How do you prove it?"

"Christine didn't have any of the supernatural energy flowing around her, but James did. He could be the primary human the ghost has attached to. But we don't have complete information yet, Let's see if the teenagers skew more toward mom or dad."

I returned to my chair, calling over my shoulder. "Bring in Jimmy."

CHAPTER FOUR

Jimmy was nervous. And every bit the 18-year-old teenager. Plus a hint of supernatural energy sprinkled around him. Fun times for me as an investigator.

"Hi Jimmy, how are you feeling?"

"Like I don't want to be here," he snapped, though with little heat.

"You don't want to get rid of the pirate ghost?"

"If that's really the problem." He mumbled the answer, his gaze glued to his high-top sneakers.

"You don't think that's the problem?"

He lifted his gaze and gave me the classic adults-are-dumb look. "Of course not."

"Then what's the problem?"

Jimmy pursed his lips.

I waited for an answer.

He blew out a breath. "Well, I don't actually know."

"You know the pirate ghost isn't the problem, but you don't know what the problem actually is?" I tried to ask like a therapist, with no inflection at all. Not sure if I failed, or if it wasn't possible to succeed with a teenager.

"I said I don't know," he snarled.

A shot of anger roiled over me, and I frowned. Teenage anger or ghost anger?

"What?" he asked, tone more conciliatory.

The anger receded, and now I was uncertain what I'd felt. Definitely supernatural energy. Maybe. Was it from Jimmy's proximity to his father? I'd have to explore that. First, I had Jimmy lead me through the timeline of the family's vacation activities. Like his parents, he told similar tales, and became upset when discussing the ghost tour, but described nothing out of the ordinary. Nor was there a surge of the supernatural energy flanking him.

"Did you and your father go off from your mother and sister at any point during the day?"

Jimmy rolled his eyes. "Not a chance."

Now I had to wonder why his family ever wanted to do a final vacation trip with their son before college. Unless he wasn't normally quite so surly. "You don't enjoy spending time with your father."

"What? No, that's not it." His sneaker-clad foot bounced on the hardwood floor like his father's had.

"What is it then?" I asked softly, as nonthreatening as I could manage.

Jimmy's pupils dilated and his face paled.

"What just went through your mind?"

"I… don't know."

"Yes, you do, Jimmy. Help me help your family. Did something happen with your father on one of the tours?"

Jimmy's expression flattened and his entire body stilled, except a twitching finger on his right hand clasped in his lap. "Nope. Everything was like I said. Can I go now?"

I wanted to push for a real response from Jimmy. Except, I knew keeping a teenager in an interview against his will wouldn't get me anywhere, so I agreed and asked him to send in his sister. Dealing with ghosts was easier than teenagers!

"Whatever," he mumbled in my general direction as he exited the room. I heard voices, softer footsteps, and then a very tentative Kelsey Mackey took the seat opposite mine.

"Hi Doctor Danger," she greeted me politely. She crossed her ankles and clasped her hands in her lap. Her fingers fidgeted while she waited for my response.

"Hi Kelsey. How are you feeling?" I asked, in part to ease her into the interview, but also because the poor girl reeked of anxiety. It didn't appear to have even a tinge of supernatural energy, which seemed odd and contrary to my proximity theory. It was, however, strong enough to lap against my protective wall like high tide.

"I'm fine," she whispered. "Worried about my family."

That was my opening to explain what I'd told her

brother and parents. She'd tell me her thoughts and memories from the vacation, with an emphasis on the ghost tour, since that was the hypothetical start to the difficulties.

Kelsey nodded when I finished and haltingly told her story. Which was frustratingly similar to her parents and brother. Until I asked the clarifying questions that had caused her brother to shut down.

"One of your family members expressed the belief that the pirate ghost isn't the problem here."

Her eyebrows jumped in shock.

"What do you think about that statement?"

"I don't know what to think about it, except it's wrong." Her vehemence struck me.

"What makes you think it's wrong?"

"Hello? We're hallucinating a freaking pirate! Of course, the pirate ghost is the problem." She rolled her eyes, just like her brother.

I bit my tongue not to respond to the childishness.

"What did they say was the problem, if not the ghost?" she asked, sounding genuinely curious.

"They didn't offer an alternative."

Kelsey harrumphed. "That would definitely be my brother, then."

I stifled a laugh. "What would make you say that?"

"You've met him. He's disagreeable, and not helpful."

"In what way?"

"In the way that big brothers are," she said, spreading her arms wide in an I-don't-know gesture.

Possibly, she couldn't articulate what she meant, so I moved on. "Did your father and brother go off on their own at any point? Especially during the ghost tour?"

Sweat broke out all over my body, causing my skin to goose pimple in the air conditioning. Some unknown bad was coming. If we didn't figure this out, people would die. I needed to find the right—

"Doctor Danger?" Kelsey's tentative voice cut through my unexplainable thoughts and unexpected anxiety.

Where was this coming from? Anxiety continued to flow over and around me. My thoughts spun in maddening circles. Something bad was coming. People would die.

The thoughts and anxiety couldn't be mine. Where were they coming from?

When I noticed Kelsey's eyes widened in terror and the insane grip she had on the cushion upon which she sat, I confirmed the source of my reaction. I inhaled deeply and isolated her anxiety that had breached my protective wall. That was a powerful reaction to my query.

"Are you okay?" I asked Kelsey while I continued to calm myself and separate from the teen's apparent emotion. My question broke through whatever Kelsey was experiencing.

"I'm fine." She released her grip on the cushion and blinked rapidly before blowing out a rush of air.

"Kelsey, do you need me to repeat my question?"

"What? No." She crossed her arms over her midsection. "Not that I recall."

"You don't recall if your father and brother went off

on their own at any time during the tours, especially the ghost tour?"

"No, they did not go off together," she stated emphatically.

Her wording struck me as wrong somehow, and I opened my mouth to reword the question.

"Thank you for your time, Doctor. I've answered your questions. I'd like to return to my family." She rose from her seat, offered a slight nod, and then fled the room, slamming the door behind her.

Her ingrained politeness combined with her complete dismissal of me almost made me chuckle. But the situation wasn't funny.

"The kids for sure know something," Dan mused.

"Everyone knows something. Except perhaps the mother," I amended. "Let's go find out what."

CHAPTER FIVE

Four unhappy expressions met us when Dan and I entered the living room from the bedroom. Mom and Dad sat on either side of Jimmy and Kelsey, with their arms around their children protectively. Not that I could blame the parents. Kelsey looked like she was struggling not to cry, and even cranky Jimmy was folded in on himself, like he'd been attacked. The parents probably thought we'd bullied their poor kids.

Christine spoke slowly and deliberately. "We hired you to help our family, not cause trauma. Please explain why you felt it necessary to push our children so much that they fled the interviews?"

I retook my seat opposite the couch, noting in my peripheral vision that Dan did the same. This was manageable. I just needed Christine to understand what was happening. "Thank you for recognizing our intent," I started, using my soothing voice. "And for offering the opportunity for us to explain what happened during the interviews." The next part would be the most challenging.

"Do you know how I became a supernatural investigator?" I asked.

Christine tilted her head. "Dan explained in one of the blog posts that you have psychic powers."

I silently begged Dan not to laugh at her understanding of my ability. "That's close," I said. "I'm what's known as a clairempath." All four family members frowned in confusion. "It's like being psychic, in a way. I not only feel others' physical and emotional states, I experience them as my own. Does that make sense?"

The parents nodded, but the kids shook their heads.

"It means that when you're anxious—" I indicated Kelsey, who flushed. "I feel that anxiety too. But, more than that, my brain thinks it's my own anxiety."

"Whoa, freaky," Kelsey said.

"That ability makes me able to get at things that other investigators can't." Both kids looked nervous now. "I don't want to go too in the weeds with this, but based on my reactions, each of you," I said, pausing for effect, "knows something you're not telling me."

The guilt from the teenagers would have knocked me over if I hadn't been prepared. It smacked against my wall of protection but the stones survived the onslaught. Even without my clairempathy, the kids' body language gave them away. Kelsey hung her head and tapped her foot on the floor. Jimmy held my gaze, but blinked rapidly and crossed his arms tightly across his chest.

James and Christine, on the other hand, were just bewildered. That was unexpected. Where was the reaction from James? Maybe he really didn't know he had ghostly energy attached to him.

"What are you talking about?" Christine asked me and then faced her family. "Do you know what she's talking about it?"

James answered no.

The kids remained silent, but continued to nervously fidget.

Interesting. Could the kids have done something?

"Jimmy, Kelsey. Do you know what Doctor Danger is talking about?" She added Mom-voice to her question, and both kids shrank in their seats. But stubbornly stayed silent.

I believed James that he wasn't aware of exactly what was going on, but the teens didn't know that I did. If one or both of them was the guilty party, I just had to draw them out. An idea surfaced on how to do that. "James, your answer of no confuses me," I stated. It had the desired effect.

Both kids stared open-mouthed at their father.

"James, do you know something?"

The lack of accusation in Christine's question amazed me. She would have made a great therapist.

James swung his head between his family, his foot tapping against the floor. "No, I don't. I mean, I don't think I do." His gaze beseeched me for assistance. "Do you know something about me that I don't?"

Time to go for the gold. "James, you are drenched in ghost energy," I said to a round of gasps. My word choice might have been hyperbolic, but he did have ghost energy around him, whether he was aware of it or not.

"What?! The ghost is haunting my husband?"

"How is that possible? What does that mean?" James asked in abject terror.

Kelsey stared daggers at Jimmy, who pointedly ignored her and nibbled at a hangnail.

I directed my next question again at James, infusing my tone with a faked touch of incredulity. "Do you expect us to believe that you had no idea the ghost had attached itself to you?"

"I don't understand. No, how would I know?" James floundered in response. "We're all having the same dreams and hallucinations. Right?" He searched his family's faces for comfort. His wife looked uncertain and his kids looked very, very guilty.

I was still unsure if the guilt I felt from fake-blaming James was from his guilt-ridden kids or just myself. Ouch. But I needed to draw someone out here.

"Look at them," I said, pointing at each teenager in turn. "Look how guilty they are. Are your children protecting you, James? I can't help you if you don't talk to me!" My last statement encompassed the teens, and I made sure to make direct eye contact with both when I made it.

Jimmy crossed and uncrossed his arms, trying to avoid

eye contact with anyone, whereas Kelsey shifted to face him head on, her face scrunched up in anger.

"If you don't tell them, I will," Kelsey shouted at her brother.

"I don't know what you're talking about." The horror on his face didn't match the sentence, as his eyes widened and his nostrils flared.

"I saw Jimmy with an old-looking bottle of alcohol." She turned to me. "Didn't you say the haunting could be from an object?"

"Alcohol? Where did you get alcohol from?" Christine interrogated her son, missing the important part of her daughter's statement.

Jimmy covered his face with his hands.

"Is that true, Jimmy?" I asked, and he didn't answer.

I directed my next question back to Kelsey. "Did you see where he got the bottle?"

"No, I didn't. I just saw him with it when we were packing to go."

"Why didn't you say something, honey?" Christine asked.

Kelsey flushed. "I didn't know what he was doing, and I didn't want to get him in trouble."

"That's nice that you support your brother," Christine said, "but these aren't healthy secrets."

"I understand that now," Kelsey retorted, in true teenager fashion.

"Where did you get the bottle from?" I asked Jimmy.

"Why are you automatically believing her?" he

answered, smug tone back in place. He crossed his arms over his chest yet again.

"Because you look very guilty," I explained and his arms dropped into his lap. "You're also coated a bit with the ghost energy as well." I glanced at James. "Not as much as your father, but still some. And neither your mother nor your sister have any ghost energy on them, despite also having the dreams and hallucinations." I refocused on Jimmy. "Do you understand what that means?"

"Um," he eloquently responded.

"It means that either you or your father, maybe even both somehow, are attached to the ghost."

"You keep talking about the ghost as if we've agreed that's real," Jimmy scoffed.

His parents and sister wore matching stunned looks. "How else do you explain what we've been seeing?" James asked his son.

"I don't know," Jimmy answered with an insolent shrug, "but ghosts aren't real. Therefore, we are not being haunted by a pirate ghost."

"Okay," I said, while frantically considering how to approach this. I'd stick with the facts. "Are you denying what your sister saw? Of you with an old-appearing bottle of alcohol?"

Jimmy stared over my shoulder a moment before responding. "No, I'm not denying that."

"Where did you get the bottle?"

"I don't remember."

"Jimmy!" Even his mother was finally exasperated.

"I don't," he insisted angrily. "I just found it."

"We're going to need a little more to go on here," I said drily.

He stared over my shoulder again.

I glanced back in that direction, too, and saw nothing. "Is the pirate appearing to you?"

"Of course not," Jimmy quickly answered.

It felt like a lie, but I couldn't demand the kid acknowledge a ghost he was adamant didn't exist.

"I don't want to get in trouble," Jimmy whispered.

"You won't, honey. We just need the truth so we can figure out what happened," his mother said, rubbing his arm.

I wasn't so sure he couldn't get in trouble, but one problem at a time.

"On the ghost tour," Jimmy started and stopped, "in one of the houses, when I left to find the bathroom, I couldn't find one. On my way back, I saw this roped-off section down one of the hallways."

"Oh Jimmy," Christine uttered, appearing crestfallen.

"I wondered what could be back there. So I ducked under the rope and wandered around." He shrugged in the dismissive way that only teenagers could. "I found a boarded-up secret compartment in a bedroom being renovated."

"How cool," Kelsey whispered.

She wasn't wrong, but we didn't need to encourage Jimmy's trespassing, disturbing antique objects, and lying about it.

"I saw the dusty old bottle and thought it would make a cool souvenir." He finished his story with a shrug, the gravity of the situation lost on him.

A dusty old bottle in an historic home? Stealing a haunted object never ended well. But at least it offered a partial explanation. "Disturbing the bottle likely brought the ghost to your family."

Christine sobbed and Jimmy's expression became an odd mix of guilt and contempt.

I stared at the teenager. "What I don't understand is why your father has the bulk of the ghost energy attached to him instead of you if you stole the bottle?"

Both parents and Jimmy flinched at my use of the word stole, but none voiced an objection.

"Do you know why, Jimmy?" I asked.

Jimmy's mouth opened and closed in an excellent imitation of a fish, but no words came out.

"Do you know?" I repeated my question in a softer tone.

Jimmy had the good graces to look sheepish. "Yeah. I put the bottle in Dad's backpack last night."

A beat of silence. Then verbal pandemonium as his family members peppered him with overlapping questions and comments, barely pausing to breathe, talking over each other, and not allowing him to respond.

"Why would you do that?"

"Not cool, bro."

"How could you?"

"I don't understand your thinking."

"What if something really bad happened?"

I held up my hands in the universal sign to shut up. "Shhh, everyone." When the room quieted, I addressed Jimmy. "What was your plan?"

"I don't know. I didn't want it to be found on me."

"What was your plan for if your father found it?"

"I don't know," he snapped. "Just that I wouldn't be found with it while you were investigating."

"That's a terrible plan," Kelsey interrupted with a bark of derisive laughter.

"Not helpful, sweetie," her mother chastised, and Kelsey quieted.

I shushed the family. "Jimmy, now that we have it, our first step will be to try returning the bottle to where you found it. Do you remember which house? Can you take us there?"

"No."

CHAPTER SIX

"James Junior, you will tell us right now which house you stole this bottle from," his mother demanded.

"I don't remember," he mumbled, his eyes darting to the side in a clear tell that he was lying.

I managed not to sigh, but this reminded me why I didn't want kids… they became teenagers. Time for some reverse psychology. "Jimmy, you're right. You don't need to tell us where you found the bottle."

"What?" James Senior spluttered.

"Yes, he does," Christine contradicted.

I ignored them and focused on Jimmy. My next nonchalant statement had to be perfect. "I mean, who cares if they're haunted to death and you become an orphan?" I shrugged. "No doubt, you have a plan." I widened my eyes theatrically. "You do have a plan, don't you?"

"Of course I do," Jimmy responded, but the fear under his bravado pushed against my wall of protection.

"What is it?" I asked, pretending to straighten my shirt while I attempted to shore up my inner defenses before his emotions breached my wall.

"I'm not telling you," he retorted.

Harnessing my inner middle school student, I lifted a hand to cup my mouth from the side and stage whispered to his parents. "He doesn't have a plan. It's fine, we can figure out which house—"

"No!" Jimmy jumped to his feet, anger rolling off of him. "You can't!"

"You're right," I agreed, wondering why I'd align myself with these idiot parents. This case was a nonstarter. There was no reason to bother with the house.

"He is?" Christine asked, her head swiveling between me and her son. She gasped, having trouble catching her breath.

I gulped in air, unable to catch my own breath, now certain I was screwing everything up. That thankfully clued me in that my protection wall had been breached. The strength and severity of the son's anger weakened me, and then his mother's anxiety just rolled on over. They were exhausting.

Several stones restacked on my wall brought relief. I faced the family. Time for some truth. "Jimmy, your anger is overwhelming, but I sense the fear beneath it. Your refusal to help is terrifying your mother to the point that she's on the verge of a panic attack. Please. I know you love your family and you don't want them to die. I need you to be honest and tell me what's happening."

Jimmy remained silent, his gaze flicking between his sister and the adults all staring at him expectantly. His right foot tapped for a moment, then stilled. The fingers on his left hand opened and closed before also stilling. He cleared his throat as if to speak, but didn't. A final deep inhale and exhale before the fidgeting stopped. "The pirate is angry and doesn't want me to help you," he blurted out and then clasped both hands over his mouth.

"Very good, Jimmy," I said, leaning forward to pat his knee. "I understand how difficult that was for you."

His hands didn't move, though he nodded.

"Can you try to tell me why the pirate doesn't want you to cooperate with your family?"

"You can't find the treasure," he squeaked out, his face contorting as if he was in physical pain.

"Pirate treasure?" his sister asked in awe. "Now that's cool."

"Enough of that nonsense," his father ordered, clearly irritated. "That's just fanciful nonsense."

Everyone stared in shock at James.

"That was a strong opinion," I said.

James reddened. "Sorry, that was weird, right? I don't know what came over me."

An intriguing thought occurred to me, but I needed more information from Jimmy first. "The pirate has told you that there is a treasure, and he doesn't want us to find it," I clarified and he nodded. "Do you know where the treasure is?" I asked out of curiosity; I didn't believe there was a treasure, but what did I know?

Jimmy swallowed and then shook his head violently, his loose locks flying back and forth across his face.

"But you believe the ghost? That there is a treasure?"

"Yes."

"Why isn't the ghost telling you where the treasure is?"

"I'm not worthy yet."

"Yet?"

Jimmy shrugged.

"When will you be worthy?" I asked, pushing a little.

"I don't know," Jimmy whispered.

Time to try something else. "Do you know the pirate's name?"

"No." Jimmy appeared surprised by his response to my question.

"Why would you do what he's asking when he hasn't bothered to trust you with his name?"

"I…" Jimmy's Adam's apple bobbed in his throat. "I don't know. He might be lying."

My gaze sharpened on his. "What makes you think that?"

"I'm not sure. Something seems different."

I glanced between James and Jimmy. "Different from what?"

"I don't know," Jimmy whispered.

"Does your mind feel less clouded?" I asked Jimmy. "Clearer than when you first arrived here."

"Kinda."

"You, on the other hand," I said to James, "I would guess are feeling more off-kilter since arriving."

"Well, yes, but that's because of the haunting. Isn't it?"

"Yes, but not for the reason you think." I stood from the chair and paced to the window, staring out into the sunny afternoon. I turned back to the family, waiting for me to explain. "Here's where I think we are. We're correct that the ghost is attached to the bottle. Jimmy's taking the bottle attached the ghost to the family, and especially to him." Jimmy dropped his head at my statement. "However, when Jimmy hid the bottle in his father's backpack, that began transferring, for lack of a better word, the ghost's anger and control more from Jimmy over to James." I tilted my head in James's direction. "That's why you had your brief outburst to protect the treasure's location."

"But the treasure is real?" Kelsey asked hopefully.

I chuckled and the tension in the room dropped a hair. "To be honest, I have no idea." Now I included Dan in my comments. "Our next step is to figure out who the pirate is."

"That one might be easier than you think," Christine said with a half-smile.

"It might?" I asked in surprise.

"The most famous missing treasure in this part of the country is Blackbeard's. He's the most logical ghost to be haunting us to protect his missing treasure."

"That's a reasonable guess," I agreed. "What do you think, Dan?"

"He's the only one I've heard of," he concurred, "so, yeah, it's a reasonable guess."

I nearly smacked my forehead. "What am I thinking? I'm wrong. Identifying the pirate, while nice, may not even be necessary for our next step."

"It's not?" Dan asked in confusion.

"Not at all."

CHAPTER SEVEN

Everyone stared at me, waiting for me to explain myself. "Remember what I said our first plan would be, once we learned of the haunted bottle?"

"You said we'd try returning the bottle to where Jimmy found it," Dan answered.

"Exactly."

Understanding dawned on the parents' faces. "It doesn't matter who the pirate is," Christine said, "if we're putting the bottle back where Jimmy found it."

"Now, if the ghost—" I couldn't bring myself to call him Blackbeard until we confirmed his identity. "—won't allow Jimmy or James to help us, then we'll need to figure it out ourselves."

"Which I believe we can do," Christine said, standing up and striding to a side table pushed against a wall near the kitchen. A brown cloth purse lay there, and she pulled a cellphone from it. "We already know it had to be one of the houses on the ghost tour. We also already know that it was one we went into that had some level of construction happening."

Her excitement was infectious. "We'll start with the list of the homes on the tour."

"Compare their descriptions to the pictures I took." Her eyes lit up. "Maybe I took a picture of a blocked-off area."

"Do you remember doing that?"

"I don't, but that doesn't mean I didn't."

James and Jimmy were looking equal parts irritated and nauseous as Christine and I had our rapid-fire exchange. They truly weren't going to be a lot of help. I wouldn't even ask them, to be honest, in case they misled us on the ghost's behalf.

Christine retrieved the ghost tour list of homes, and she, Dan, and I squeezed onto the couch, displacing James and the teens.

"What can I do?" Kelsey asked, twisting a lock of hair around her finger.

"Keep an eye on your brother and father. Maybe in the kitchen," I answered, happy to see both James and Jimmy follow Kelsey out of the room without complaint. Maybe with the ghost's energy still transferring between Jimmy and James, the ghost couldn't fully latch onto one or the other and their real selves could guide them.

An ugly thought rose in my mind. "If we just return

the bottle to where Jimmy found it, what happens to the next person who finds it?"

Dan frowned. "They'll become the next haunting victims."

"What does that mean for our plan?" Christine asked, worry for the next family clear in her voice.

I thought for a moment. There had to be a solution. We couldn't just return the bottle to where Jimmy found it and hope nobody else stumbled upon it. That would be incredibly irresponsible. But we needed to get the bottle away from the Mackey family before the hostile energy consumed them. I snapped my fingers.

"You have a brilliant idea," Dan said.

"I don't know how brilliant it is, but I have a workable idea. Our plan just became a two-parter."

"Step one?" Dan asked.

"What we're already planning. We bring the bottle back to where Jimmy found it."

Dan nodded his head. "Returning it to its home will release the hold it has on the family."

"Exactly," I said.

"Thank goodness," Christine interjected. "What's the second part, then?"

"We figure out how to deactivate, for lack of a better word, the ghost himself," I said, as bile rose in my throat and I gripped my upper thighs. This time I had suspected the ghost would try something, and I reinforced my barrier.

"Sarah?" Dan asked.

"Our ghost doesn't like the plan," I bit out. Suddenly,

the emotion drained from me. And the pirate ghost stood in the arched doorway to the bedroom.

His intense blue eyes stared out from his youthful face. He waved an arm at me, his white puffy sleeve fluttering. One hip jutted out, and he drew circles on the floor with the toe of his left boot. The nonchalance struck me as staged, but I couldn't figure out why.

"I do not care about thy plan," the ghost tittered. "You've no idea what you face."

"Tell me then, Blackbeard," I said, trying out the name. If the ghost responded to the use of the name, physically or emotionally, I couldn't tell. And that meant I still didn't know if we were right about his identity.

"Why would I do that?" he sneered.

"To show how much smarter you are?"

"'Tis already clear."

"Is it now?"

"Ye scallywag landlubber," he said, taking two steps closer and pointing a dirty finger at me. "As I said, this will be fun."

The ghost vanished.

After I caught Dan and Christine up on the pirate's side of the conversation, we doubled down on figuring out which house Jimmy had stolen the bottle from. It was quicker than we thought. The list of houses on the tour mentioned that a newly discovered one had a pirate history and they'd begun restoring sections not yet visited on the tour.

"That one seems the most likely," I said.

"Let me see what pictures I have from that house." Christine scrolled through the apparent hundreds of photos on her phone from their trip. "Bingo." She held the phone out to me. "That's the house. Do you see what I see?" She showed me a picture of ornate wallpaper. To the right of the wall, in the background, a red rope barred a hallway.

"This is the house added to the tour?"

"I believe so," she said.

"What do we know about the house?"

Dan tapped into his tablet, searching, while Christine read from the map of homes she'd gotten on the tour. Between the two of them, we pieced together what we learned.

The home was named the Knight House, after Tobias Knight, the secretary of the colony from 1712, although research was unclear which of his descendants had owned the house. The property had recently sold and the new owners found unspecified evidence of Knight in the home, even though it seemed that the known Tobias Knight descendants weren't involved. That had prompted much speculation about a mistress and her babes, but in any event, the new owners reported strange noises, lights, and smells throughout the building. They'd planned to demolish the red brick, single-story home, but it was in better shape than they'd expected.

The evidence of haunting led them to speak with ghost tour operators about adding the home instead. Both the map's information and online sources confirmed that the house had been renovated in sections, and was on the final room.

"This last bedroom undergoing renovations must be where Jimmy snagged the bottle," I concluded. Dan and Christine agreed.

"Now what?" Dan asked.

"Bring me the bottle." I flashed a mischievous smile. "We're going on a field trip."

CHAPTER EIGHT

My preference was to drive. I loved my dark blue Subaru
Forester Sport. It came in handy whether I needed to haul
large supernatural objects or, in this case, part of one
haunted family. Dan drove so I could examine the bottle
on our way to the Knight House, Savannah's newest
haunted home. Christine accompanied us, but James and
the teens stayed behind. That was for two reasons. One, we
didn't know what impact the ghostly presence could have
if James and Jimmy, specifically, were there. Two, larger
groups were more conspicuous.

The bottle was an almost black glass, with a wide, but
squat height, and a moderate-length neck. When I gave a
gentle shake, I swore I heard something move, but it didn't
sound like liquid. Nor could it be, when it wasn't sealed.
Of course, any cork used to seal it was long gone, but even

shining my pocket flashlight into the opening failed to reveal its contents. Maybe because of the darkness of the glass? I wasn't sure.

Christine remained quiet in the backseat as Dan drove, until we'd nearly reached The Pirate's House. "We had lunch here," she piped up from behind us. "It might be the oldest haunted building in Savannah." She pointed ahead. "Once we pass the Trustee Garden, the Knight House is also on the right, before East Bay Street. You'll want to either park in the lot here by the Garden, or see if there's an open spot on the street ahead."

"I see someone pulling out," Dan said and drove forward, snagging the spot.

"Rock star parking," I said with a smile and opened the door. I'd placed the haunted bottle in a plastic bag found in the vacation rental's kitchen. Since it wasn't oversized, my hope was it would look like we'd purchased something at a gift shop, and nobody working in the Knight House would ask about the contents.

The three of us exited the car and stood before the small, red brick, single-story home. It certainly looked like an 18th-century building. Christine, standing next to me, shivered.

"Are you okay?" I asked.

She nodded but didn't speak.

We walked up the cracked sidewalk to the simple Colonial-style home and through the open door. An older woman with a short pixie cut sat at a wooden desk situated just off the immediate entrance.

"Welcome to the Knight House," she greeted us with a smile. "The home is small enough to tour on your own, if you'd like that information."

"Yes, thank you very much," I said and accepted the offered trifold. A picture of the home graced the front, and when opened, a map of the small home was laid out inside. Stars on the map matched with descriptions on the bottom of the page, summarizing the room and the haunting indicators, such as unexplained ghostly apparitions and laughing. There was also a very limited paragraph summary on the back of the trifold, providing scant information about the provenance of the home. That information matched what we'd already learned.

The 7-foot tall ceiling in the front room might have been claustrophobic for taller folks, but for me, at only 5'2", I was good. A glance at Dan showed he was okay, but Christine looked pale. How much that had to do with just being here, though, was hard to say. We knew from Jimmy that we were looking for the part of the home roped off for renovation. We moved with purpose through the small, connected rooms, mostly ignoring the highlighted features, such as the brick chimney and the original smallish windows.

At the back of the home, we hit pay dirt. As Jimmy told us and the picture captured, down a hall on the right side of the home, a red rope and sign informed visitors that this room was sadly unavailable, as it was under renovation. The stanchions blocked access to what looked like a bedroom. Workers had spread a plastic tarp out over the heart pine flooring, protecting it from boots and dropped equipment. The room otherwise appeared bare from the doorway.

"I don't see what Jimmy was talking about," I muttered and leaned over the rope, twisting side to side. And then I saw it. In a back corner, not immediately visible from the doorway, hung another plastic tarp, blocking a hole in the wall. I glanced behind us, didn't see anybody else in this part of the home, and hopped the red rope.

Or at least attempted to hop the rope. My established clumsiness rose up, and I went down. With the rope. I winced in anticipation of the metal poles that held up the rope crashing down beside me.

"I got them," Dan said, with a wink, holding one pole aloft, which stretched out the red rope to keep the pole on the other end from hitting the floor.

"Nice work." I scrambled to my feet, brushing dust and grime off of my jeans while I surreptitiously scanned our surroundings to see if anyone might have seen or heard my spill.

"I'm always ready, doc," Dan said, resetting the poles.

"Christine, can you stand watch?" I asked. We didn't need a guard; after all, what would she do if someone challenged her? The place was too small. Really, I just didn't want her in the room. Her heightening anxiety thumped hard against my protective wall.

Christine's relieved nod told me I'd made the right call.

Dan stepped over the red rope, joining me in the

small, dusty bedroom. We crossed the floor, our shoes crinkling on the plastic, until we stood before the covered wall. In this back, left corner, we could no longer see Christine standing just outside the room.

"What next?"

"Shut up and let me think," I snapped.

"Uh-huh," came his response.

"The ghost knows we're here," I said by way of apology, before focusing inward to shore up my flagging protective wall.

"Do you think that anger is coming directly from the ghost or channeling through Christine? I mean, she's not even in here."

"Not sure. This is unfamiliar territory." I peeled the plastic back and peered into the not-exactly-cavernous hole it was covering. Someone had previously put a one-inch false wall made of plaster into the room. Nobody noticed, I surmised, because it had been covered with wallpaper. I imagined workers found it when they realized the overall wall thickness was too much for what it was. "Do you think they'll widen this hole? Really play up its possible relation to the house's haunting?" I mused.

"If they're smart," he answered.

"Hold this, please."

Dan held the plastic back so that I could enter the space. I braced myself for a ghostly encounter, but nothing happened. Either our ghost wasn't aware yet that we were here, or he didn't care. That bothered me; if he didn't care, that meant we were on the wrong track.

A handful of additional bottles sat on three shelves lining the back of the closet-sized enclosure. Layers of dust covered them and an involuntary shudder ran through me that a ghost might be attached to each one. Surely not.

"Moment of truth," I whispered, retrieving the bottle from the plastic bag and setting it in a spot that looked suspiciously clean of dust. "If we're correct, this should do the trick."

"How do you feel?"

I probed over and around my wall, and my heart sank when I still felt supernatural emotion. In fact, the crawling sense of ghostly energy was unchanged. We knew we'd likely have to deactivate the bottle too, but this step should have produced a reduction in the supernatural emotion. Or at least, that had been our hypothesis. With a frown, I said, "Let's check in with Christine. I don't feel any different, but I'm not a member of the haunted family."

"True. But, if this solved the haunting, you should feel the removal of unnatural emotion, right?" He tried for a neutral tone, but I guessed he believed as I did. Our plan might not work.

I stepped back into the bedroom and Dan allowed the plastic to fall into place behind me. We paced across the room to join Christine in the doorway.

"What happened? Did you put it back?" she asked, wringing her hands.

"We did," I answered. "How do you feel?"

Her eyes closed for a moment, and when they opened, a sheen of moisture gleamed, accenting her brown eyes.

Uh-oh, that wasn't good. Was she about to cry?

"I feel the same. I don't feel any different." Her voice rose on the last word, a note of hysteria creeping in.

I was better prepared this time and blocked off that anxious hysteria from my own mind. Except—

Thank goodness I'd blocked myself, as a wave of the pirate ghost's hallmark gleeful malevolence swept over me, threatening to drown me.

"Oh my," Christine squealed, her eyes darting to a spot over my shoulder.

I turned, dread pooling in my belly at what I knew I'd find. Sure enough, the insolent pirate leaned against the back window, the covering not acknowledged by the spectral intruder. He grinned with uneven, yellowing teeth.

"Did ye think it would be that easy?" he sneered.

"You can see him too," Christine said in shock.

I realized this was the first time we'd both seen him at the same time. "Why can we both see you?" I asked him.

"'Tis where that boy snatched me bottle." The pirate opened his mouth as if to say more, but then gave a little finger wag at us and closed his mouth again.

Wave after wave of anger washed over me. It became a struggle to control. "I won't be able to stay here much longer," I spat out between gritted teeth.

Dan grabbed my elbow to lead me away. "Then we leave. Now."

While I appreciated his protectiveness, we were about to commit a huge mistake. "Not without the bottle."

Before I could make a move, Christine vaulted the red

rope and raced to the covered hole in the wall. She yanked the plastic aside, reached in to grab the bottle that caused all the trouble, and ran back to us in the doorway. She slid it into the plastic bag. At that, the pirate winked out of our plane of existence.

A loud cackling filled my head, and I saw Christine wince, so knew he was giving us a parting gift.

Dan couldn't hear the ghost, but he saw our reactions to it, so he reached for Christine with his other hand. "We need to get out of here now."

Our trio headed back toward the front of the house. We'd hoped to exit without interaction, but the woman at the desk gave us a probing look and asked, "How was it? Did you see or hear anything odd?"

I wondered what she'd heard. Dropping my voice to a stage whisper, I answered, truthfully, "We heard a ghost laughing."

She nodded as if that was an everyday occurrence, and then confirmed that it often was. "We're still not sure what happened here. You should come back when we have the renovations done."

"Not likely," Christine muttered, nearly throwing herself out the door.

At the volunteer's frown, I tried to explain. "She came for us; she's not big on hauntings."

"Of course. It's not for everyone," the woman said. "Have a good rest of your day."

At that, Dan and I made our escape outside to join Christine gulping breaths of fresh air.

"Do you go through this stuff all the time? I don't know how you do it," Christine said when we reached her.

"It's not usually quite like this," I assured her as we walked to the SUV.

Once inside, Dan faced me. "Where to?"

"I don't know," I admitted. We didn't have a Plan B and I didn't know how to deactivate the bottle. "Time to call in reinforcements."

CHAPTER NINE

Back in our vacation rental after dropping Christine off at hers, Dan and I stared at the tablet screen, where Amanda Jenkins smiled out at us. She was the team's researcher. Her background in library science combined with her facility with computers made her the perfect part-time researcher. And, since Mandie was also married and mother to four kids under the age of 13, she had zero interest in accompanying us on our work trips.

We'd prepped for the call by typing up our notes on the case thus far, and taking photos of the bottle from every angle to text to Mandie.

Dan had set the squat glass bottle on the edge of the kitchen table. I'd tipped it in different directions for the photographs, plus placed my phone against it for the size reference. Once all of that was complete, we'd sat next to each other on one side of the table, and video-called Mandie to update her.

"That's fascinating," she said now, in response to our summary of the trip. "Send me those pics of the bottle and I'll work on confirming its age."

"Perfect. Dan will do that now," I said, with a glance in his direction.

He started typing on his phone.

"We'll do our own internet sleuthing," I continued. "We've been told the major missing treasure around here is Blackbeard's, but it would be nice to confirm that."

"Does the pirate ghost you've seen look like Blackbeard?" she asked.

I shrugged. "He's a youngish-looking dark-haired pirate. I'm honestly not sure. I did a quick check before calling you and the images are all paintings similar to the ghost I've seen. None of them are identical, of course, since there are no actual photographs of Blackbeard."

Mandie laughed, her hazel eyes twinkling. "That would be too easy, right? He was about a hundred years too early for that, I believe."

"I believe you're right," I concurred. With another glance at Dan, who gave me a thumbs up, I continued. "Did you get the photos?" When Mandie confirmed that the photos were good enough to research, we said our goodbyes, with a plan to touch base after an early lunch.

Dan made us vegetable sandwiches from the well-stocked kitchen and then we returned to the kitchen table.

"Ready to see what we can find?" I asked Dan,

handing him his tablet and retrieving my laptop from my backpack.

"You know it."

Silence descended except for the clacking of keys as we searched the wilds of the internet for missing treasure in the Georgia area. It turned out that people were both right and wrong about Blackbeard's treasure.

Tybee Island, just off the coast of Savannah, was a known pirate hangout. The rumor was that a bunch of pirates, possibly including Blackbeard, used it as a hideout from the authorities and to stash their loot. Treasure hunters and tourists had found coins on the beaches of the island, but no big scores that we could find. It wasn't that big of an island, though, so the chances of an undiscovered treasure physically there seemed remote; plus we didn't find the names of other pirates.

St. Simons Island also was rumored to be the home to missing Spanish coins after pirates ran the Spanish off. These stories suggested scattered coins, not a consolidated treasure, so assuming the pirate was telling the truth—a big if, for sure—it seemed to be another dead end.

We also found tales of missing gold hidden by members of the Cherokee Nation on Face Mountain and at F.R. Groover Farm, but since our ghost was a pirate, these seemed unlikely angles. There were other stories of missing gold, but most of these occurred after our pirate timeframe, so also unlikely to be related.

There turned out to be quite a few tales of hidden loot in the 1800s, but these also occurred after authorities had predominantly contained piracy. One of my favorites was the twelve wooden kegs filled with hundreds of thousands of dollars in gold coins that got, shall we say, *misplaced* and never seen again. Irrelevant to our current case, but it made me laugh to consider that the kegs were still considered missing. I suspected someone stole the money back in the day and spent it slowly to prevent recognition for what it was. Smart thieves.

While entertaining, by the time Dan and I finished our searching, we'd concluded that Blackbeard's treasure was the only one of note to be missing. And Blackbeard was really the only notable pirate for the Savannah area. All the other names we found were Blackbeard's crew, or they were fictional, like Captain Flint and Billy Bones in Robert Louis Stevenson's *Treasure Island,* or Black Dog in the Muppet version.

Regarding Blackbeard's crew, we found a list from 1718. According to the records, authorities hung fourteen for piracy and most of the rest died in battle alongside Blackbeard. We considered whether one of his crew members was our ghost. It seemed unlikely that one of the two dozen men would know the treasure's hidden location and want to protect it enough to stay connected as a ghost. It, therefore, seemed unlikely to be a crew member.

And, finally, it was also possible that another, more obscure, pirate was our ghost, but it seemed even more unlikely that an unknown pirate had a missing treasure of note. We were confident we had our ghost's identity.

Blackbeard, born Edward Teach in 1680, was a

notorious English pirate active during the so-called Golden Age of Piracy in the early 18th century. He died in battle in 1718 off the coast of Ocracoke Island, North Carolina. We discovered several ghost stories connected to Blackbeard, including that he still haunted North Carolina, looking for his decapitated head.

Ouch.

We read quite a bit about whether there was even evidence of a missing treasure. Historians didn't believe that there was a missing treasure. Most felt this was a mythology manufactured for fictional interest (thank you, *Treasure Island!*).

That there might not be an actual treasure was, in fact, likely. Ghosts stuck in our plane often became confused. It was possible that our pirate unknowingly created a story about his lost treasure.

But, if Blackbeard died off the coast of a North Carolina island, why was his ghost attached to a bottle in Savannah?

CHAPTER TEN

A glance at the clock told me it was time to reconnect with Mandie, review what we'd learned, and decide our next steps. Dan set his tablet up and we initiated a video chat.

"Hey team," Mandie greeted us from offscreen. Her curly brown hair bobbed as she plopped down in front of the tablet.

"Hope you had as productive a time as we did," I said, by way of greeting. "What have you learned?"

"Based on the pictures alone—since I obviously can't vouch for its physical nature from just images—the bottle appears to be consistent with the most active of pirate times," she said.

"That's great." I held the squat glass bottle in my hands. "Were you able to narrow down the timeframe?"

"Not really. It's definitely consistent with bottles used

for liquor in the 1700s, the so-called Golden Age of Piracy, but it has a wider use history as well."

"Hmm, that's too bad, but not unexpected," I said.

"Right. Liquor has been popular for a long time," Mandie joked.

"We're certainly fans," Dan agreed.

"And we'll celebrate with some later," I said with a chuckle. "Let me bring you up to speed with what we learned, Mandie."

When I finished, Mandie summarized our findings. "It sounds like Blackbeard as our pirate is the most reasonable hypothesis. And he might be a bit confused about the existence of a treasure."

"Precisely," Dan said.

"The next question is, how has he latched onto the bottle enough to haunt an entire family? To the point of hallucinations, even changing their motivations and behavior?" I placed the squat bottle on the kitchen table and eyed it uneasily. "How long before that haunting transfers to us, since we have physical possession of the bottle?"

"Yeah, this is more than a typical haunting." Mandie frowned. "I've never heard of anything like it. None of the family members have exhibited supernatural tendencies in the past?"

I shook my head. "They've said no."

"So the chances of one of them enhancing the ghost's power is small," Mandie concluded.

"Close to zero," I agreed.

"What else could enhance the ghost's power?" Dan asked, removing his frameless eye glasses to pinch his nose.

The three of us chewed on that question for a moment.

"Even without an additional supernatural component," Mandie said, "negative energy can enhance a ghost's power."

"I think we're safe to eliminate that one. The family had just finished a successful vacation when the changes began." An undefinable feeling probed me, like icicles in my mind, and I eyed the bottle again. A quick grab then I shoved it back into the plastic bag.

"Out of sight, out of mind," Dan said with a snort.

"I hope so," I said, and explained to Mandie the action she'd missed offscreen.

"What about witchcraft of some sort?" Mandie asked.

I nodded slowly. "Maybe. The bottle could have a spell attached."

"But," Dan said, "don't those usually require active reinforcement?"

"In other words, if a witch cast a spell, how would it still be active hundreds of years later?" I asked.

"Exactly."

"It varies," I said, "which I know is an unhelpful answer. Some spells do, and so would either end with the witch's death or fade over time. But some enchantments can last pretty long."

"So, there could be a witch's spell involved?" Mandie clarified.

"Could be. I recall from my studies that Earth magic was actually common in the Colonies." I pulled my laptop closer and typed a question about spells in the 1700s. "According to the internet, I recalled correctly. It wasn't uncommon for so-called folk magic to be practiced alongside Christianity. Of course, most of that wasn't truly supernatural. Let me try to narrow that down." I typed a more specific query about casting spells in 1700s Savannah. "Ohh."

"What?" Mandie asked as Dan leaned over to read my screen.

"Of course," he said. "Voodoo. Why didn't we think of that?"

"That's why we research," I reminded him with a nudge and we shared a smile.

Mandie's head dipped, and I heard her typing across the line. "Yep, that part of the country actively practiced voodoo."

"How involved were pirates in voodoo?" I wondered aloud and joined Mandie in typing.

Mandie chuckled. "All the responses relate to a certain super-popular pirate movie series."

"I see that," I agreed, biting my lip as I considered how to narrow it down. "Adding Savannah to my query eliminated the movie references and brought up more relevant hits."

"Me too." Mandie scanned her screen. "There we go."

I ceased typing. "What?"

"I searched, What pirates practiced voodoo?"

"And?" I asked, though her gleeful smile told me my answer.

"Blackbeard," she said in triumph.

"Nice." I typed a few other related queries. "Interesting…"

"Share with the class, please," Mandie prompted.

"According to this, Blackbeard's use of voodoo alienated him from other pirates. That suggests it wasn't widespread at all within piracy and lends more support to our ghost being Blackbeard."

"And that he used voodoo to attach his energy to this bottle? But for what purpose? To gift his treasure to someone worthy? What does that even mean?" Dan asked in an apparent stream-of-consciousness bit of questioning. He might have identified the crux of this haunting, however.

I grabbed the side of my head. "What are we even doing? There's no point now. We can't undo a voodoo curse." A blinding pain shot through my head and I leaned over my knees.

"Sarah!" came shouts from Mandie and Dan, though muted.

That earlier sensation of icicles in my brain became an entire blizzard of wind, snow, and ice. I gritted my teeth. This was ridiculous. We knew nothing about voodoo. Giving up and going home made the most—

Oh, I don't think so, Blackbeard.

I leaped to my feet. "Show yourself, ghost. I know that's you in my head."

A shimmer to my right and then Blackbeard appeared, all crazed smiles. He leaned back against the far kitchen counter. "Did ye like me trick?"

"Trick?" I asked, before understanding dawned and my eyes widened.

"Ye savvy now." He withdrew a blade from its scabbard, brandished it at me in a mock-threatening way, and then resheathed it.

"How are you doing that?" The ghost had figured out my clairempathy and projected what he wanted me to experience. I wasn't feeling *his* physical and emotional experience. I was feeling what he *wanted* me to. That had never happened before.

He shrugged insolently. "Didn't think it would work. Figured it was worth a try, though. Good luck breaking me curse." He winked back out of our plane.

The ghost thought he was so smart. Using my own ability against me. So smugly certain that we couldn't break his unbreakable curse. I spun to face Dan, who lifted the tablet so I could see Mandie too.

"What's the plan?" Mandie asked.

"Time to break a pirate's voodoo curse," I replied grimly.

CHAPTER ELEVEN

"Is this the right place?" Dan asked uncertainly.

"I believe so. She doesn't advertise her services." The single-story brick home before us was unprepossessing. Stepping onto the wooden porch, a glance up confirmed we were likely in the right place. The ceiling color was a pale blue-green. If I was correct, the color was *haint* blue. This was a Southern variation of the word *haunt*. Since ghosts were not believed to be able to cross water, the use of the color prevented ghosts from entering the premises. It wasn't as common as it had been years ago, but its presence here suggested we had found the home we were looking for.

The woman who opened the door grinned at us, showing a gap in her white teeth. "You must be Doctor Danger and Daniel? Jeff said to expect you."

I only knew the bare minimum about voodoo from one course in my doctoral program. That wouldn't remotely be enough information to identify and break a curse. We needed an outside expert. A quick consult with our former boss, Jeff McCarthy, pointed us to the local expert now standing in the doorway.

"Priestess Lowell? It's a pleasure to meet you," I responded, extending my hand.

A throaty laugh met my greeting. "Please, call me Marie. Priestess is more for voodoo practitioners than hoodoo."

"My apologies," I said.

"No need. It's a common occurrence." Marie spun, her flowing, brightly colored dress matching her movement.

We followed her through the doorway and past the cozy living room while she continued to educate us.

"Hoodoo is more of a folk magic practiced in the South, whereas voodoo is an acknowledged religion practiced throughout the world, and largely concentrated in Louisiana, here in the States. But there are similarities."

"How do you know Jeff?" Dan asked, and another throaty laugh followed.

"He got into a bit of a scrape here a few years ago and I helped him out." She looked over her shoulder long enough to wink at us.

"That's not surprising," I said with my own chuckle.

Marie passed through her small kitchen and into a square room scented with incense. The room was filled

with candles, herbs, oils, tarot cards, and empty sachets—
likely waiting for the ingredients to create a mojo or
conjure bag to help a client.

"Jeff said that you need help with a haunted object?"
Marie asked, her dark eyes serious.

"Yes, ma'am," I answered, retrieving the bottle from
the plastic bag, its apparent permanent home for the
duration of this case.

She accepted the glass bottle from me, tilting it this
way and that, examining the piece. After that, she closed
her eyes and simply held the bottle. Her eyes flashed a
warning when she reopened them. "This is dark magic."

"Yes," I agreed and explained what had been
happening to the Mackey family.

"That sounds like a curse," Marie concluded after my
summary.

"That's what we were afraid of. We tried to replace the
bottle where it had been found, but not only did that not
work, the ghost taunted us for our failure."

Deep lines formed around Marie's frown. "Powerful
dark magic," she amended her original conclusion. "I don't
believe a purifying bath will work, nor an uncrossing spell,"
she continued, although she seemed to be working through
the options more for herself. "A binding may work, but we
may need something stronger to break the curse."

"Can you help us break the curse?" Dan interrupted
her musings with his question.

She inclined her head. "If you know the identity of the
conjurer, yes."

Hope soared that we would be able to free the Mackeys from Blackbeard's haunting. "The pirate Blackbeard."

Marie quirked an eyebrow at the name.

"It may sound unbelievable, but we believe so," I said.

"We will find out soon enough." Marie headed to a far corner of the room. She set the bottle on a wooden table tucked in that corner and indicated we should sit at the two chairs on either side of it. "I'll get what I need."

Marie moved through the space with the ease of someone who had done it a thousand times before. She knew exactly where to go in the crowded room to get the supplies that would break the curse.

Arms now laden with those supplies, she set up the table with the practiced movements of an expert. Black tapered candle in the middle. A stoppered bottle of what appeared to be water, so probably holy water for cleansing, next to the cursed rum bottle. And, finally, a cluster of leaves covered in tiny hairs that had a serrated margin and branching stems, next to the candle.

Marie lit the black candle. She held one leaf over it and as the scent of sweet mint filled the room, she recited a spell. "Blackbeard, you have made this cursed bottle. We banish your curse. Today, we claim a blessed cure for the Mackey family. We ask for a spiritual cleansing." As the candle continued to burn, she blew out the blackened mint leaves and dropped them in a small ceramic bowl. She pulled the stopper from the bottle of water and splashed some onto the rum bottle, repeating the spell.

However, I noticed she frowned as she finished. She blew out the candle and faced us with sad eyes. "It did not work."

"How do you know?" Dan asked, not challenging her assertion, but with a tone of genuine curiosity.

"I can still feel the dark energy," she answered.

"What happened?" I asked, worry washing over me, both from myself and from Marie's response to the failed spell.

"Blackbeard is not the one who cursed this bottle," she said with finality.

A crushing defeat engulfed me. "How is that possible?" I ran through all of our research. We'd been so confident. "Wait!" I sat up straight and actually snapped my fingers. "His given name was Edward Teach. Could it somehow be under that name instead of Blackbeard?"

Marie considered my question. "It's possible. Especially if he was baptized or otherwise known under that name to the spiritual world. Yes, it's possible."

"Then we can try it again?" I asked, desperate for this to work for the Mackey family.

"Yes," Marie said. She broke off the burned tip of the black candle and emptied the ceramic bowl of the charred mint leaves. Muttering something under her breath, she relit the candle and repeated her steps. As the fresh mint leaf burned, she said, "Edward Teach, you have made this cursed bottle. We banish your curse. Today, we claim a blessed cure for the Mackey family. We ask for a spiritual cleansing."

The soaring disappointment I felt from Marie told me the spell had failed again even before she uttered the words.

"It didn't work, did it?" Dan asked, his gaze moving from me to Marie and back again. He didn't possess supernatural gifts, but I imagined Marie and I telegraphed the answer on both our faces.

"No, it did not," Marie said. She took my hands in hers, the skin papery against mine. "I am sorry for the family you're trying to help."

"What can we do?" I begged Marie for an answer. I refused to let the pirate ghost win and torment the family, possibly to their deaths.

"Figure out who placed the curse and come back to see me."

An echo of ghostly laughter chortled in response.

CHAPTER TWELVE

Back at the large kitchen table in our rental, Dan and I began a video chat with Mandie. We updated her on the epic failure of our visit with Marie Lowell to break the pirate's curse.

"What's our next play?" Dan asked.

"The good news is that we eliminated Blackbeard as our ghost," I said with a wink. "The bad news is that we need to reconsider our assumptions that led to the wrong conclusion that Blackbeard was our ghost."

"Back to square one?" Mandie asked.

"Not quite." I pulled up my notes on my laptop and scanned what I'd typed. "Our research found that most pirates didn't practice voodoo or hoodoo." I glanced at Dan and Mandie. "Is there any reason to believe this isn't correct?"

"On it, boss," Mandie said, and I knew she immediately started querying the internet for either confirmation of that finding or something contradictory.

"Do you want some juice?" Dan asked, standing from the table.

"Sure, thanks, that would be great." I continued to scan, to decide on the next conclusion to reinvestigate.

Dan opened a cupboard and retrieved two glasses. While he poured pineapple juice into them, Mandie's head popped back into view.

"I believe we're solid on this one. Everything I'm seeing states that Blackbeard's affinity for voodoo alienated him from other pirates," she said.

"In that case," I responded slowly, reading my notes. "I think our next conclusion to revisit is that none of his crewmembers is the ghost."

"How come?" Dan asked, retaking his seat at the table and handing me my glass of juice.

I took a quick sip. Ah, that tasted refreshing. "Our original conclusion was that the ghost wasn't likely to be one of Blackbeard's crew. It seemed unlikely that one of his crewmembers would know the location of the hidden treasure and feel strongly enough about protecting it to stay connected as a ghost."

"That still seems logical," Mandie said, screwing up her mouth in thought. "But knowing most pirates were uncomfortable with voodoo and that the ghost definitely isn't Blackbeard, process of elimination leads us to it having to be one of his crew."

"Exactly." I pulled up the crew list from 1718 that we'd found. "He had hundreds of crewmembers. How do we narrow that down to identify our ghost?"

"If we presume there's an actual treasure that existed at some point," Dan began, "who among the crew would know where it is? Surely they all wouldn't."

"Depends, I suspect." I sipped my juice, thinking this through. "But we might not need to figure that piece out."

"What do you mean?" Mandie asked.

"Let's assume they all knew where the hypothetical treasure was. Who would not just attach themselves to a bottle because of it, but would actually curse the finder of the bottle?"

Dan and Mandie shrugged in tandem, not following my line of thinking.

I continued my Socratic questioning. "Let's break that down. Who would think of placing a curse on Blackbeard's treasure at all?"

Dan snapped his fingers. "Nobody would, while Blackbeard was still alive."

I pointed my right-hand index finger at Dan and placed my left-hand index finger on my nose. "Bingo."

Understanding dawned on Mandie's face. "As long as Blackbeard was alive, it was his treasure. Our ghost most likely is a member of Blackbeard's crew who outlived him."

"There weren't many, were there? That should narrow this to a handful at most," Dan said excitedly.

The three of us pulled up notes or typed into search engines, seeking that detail.

"Most of his crew died in that final battle off the coast of North Carolina," I said, reading my notes.

"And authorities hung fourteen for piracy in the immediate aftermath," Mandie added. "So they didn't have time to place a curse."

"Two men survived the battle and were acquitted of piracy charges," Dan shouted in triumph. "It's got to be one of those two men."

"Samuel Odel and Israel Hands." I had reached the same section of my notes and filled in the names. "What do we know about them?"

"Okay," Mandie said, her eyes scanning her computer screen. "Samuel Odel was released without going through a trial." More scanning. "It looks like he might have been swept up in the battle and subsequent charges because of being in the wrong place at the wrong time."

"That would be spectacularly bad timing," I joked.

"Indeed." Mandie scanned more text and then she snort-laughed. "Depending on the account, he either wanted a quick ride, or he was there to drink and play cards, then couldn't get off the ship before the battle started."

I joined in her laughter. "Okay, yeah, I'll agree he's most likely not our ghost since he doesn't seem to be a legitimate Blackbeard crewmember. Tell me about the other man."

"Israel Hands." Mandie nodded. "This sounds promising. He was Blackbeard's sailing master, or second in command."

"He'd certainly know where any treasure was. If he outlived the rest of the crew…" I frowned. "Why wouldn't he just go get it and live off of it? Why would he curse it?"

"Not sure." Mandie shrugged. "This says he returned to England and died a penniless beggar."

"If he's a dead end too, no pun intended, then we're back to square one," I muttered in frustration. "We need more information about him."

"Is it possible that he didn't go back to England?" Dan asked.

"Yes! Of course. That would be the perfect cover, wouldn't it?" I stood from the table to pace as I thought this through. Dan held his tablet aloft so Mandie could also follow my movements.

"If Israel Hands was acquitted, and was the only surviving member of the crew, he alone would know where any treasure was. If he started the story that he returned to England—and, heck, he also could have started the rumor that he died a penniless beggar—that would give him the freedom to recover and re-hide any treasure."

Dan picked up my thread of thinking. "Once he had it stashed away, he might have put the curse on it then, to keep anyone else from stealing it from him."

"It's quite brilliant," I said. "We're pretty smart for a bunch of interfering interlopers." I scowled at Dan and Mandie, whose mouths dropped open.

CHAPTER THIRTEEN

"Honestly," I continued, snarling my words and pointing at Dan and screen-Mandie. "Why we think we should be involved in any of this is ridiculous." Now I stood with hands fisted on my hips so as not to punch a hole in the kitchen wall. "I mean, honestly, none of this involves us. If we'd just back off, nature would take its course and—"

"Sarah!" Dan's yell interrupted my fuming.

"What?" I bit off my question.

"That's not you, Sarah," Mandie added. The worry in her tone popped my raging irritation.

"Oh no," I said before slumping back into a kitchen chair, cradling my head. "Give me a minute, guys." The thoughts and emotions swirled like a maelstrom. I needed to kick out the pirate's contribution and take control. With great focus, I slowly added stone after stone to my wall of protection, while also isolating the anger and derision. I surrounded the negative emotions in bubbles that I then released from my mind. As my racing heartbeat calmed and I no longer wanted to scream at my teammates, my phone pinged an incoming text. Then another. Then the phone rang. My clammy palm struggled to grip my phone as I picked up my cell from the table.

"Oh no," I repeated, reading the text as the phone pinged a recorded voicemail message. I explained to Dan and Mandie, "It's Christine and James—shoot, and even Kelsey—messaging to ask what's happening." A brick formed in my stomach. I typed a response while I continued talking. "They're all experiencing severe flashes of anger, and they think Jimmy's seeing the pirate right now."

"How is that possible?" Mandie asked.

At the same time, Dan questioned, "We have the bottle. How can the ghost be affecting both them and you?"

"Are the two of you feeling or seeing anything?" I asked in response. At the negative shakes of their heads, I frowned. "This is a huge guess, but the ghost is attached to the family, despite my having the bottle. The fact that the two of you aren't experiencing anything makes me suspect the bottle's presence here is less of an issue than my clairempathy allowing the ghost to affect me." A new set of dings sounded on my phone.

A clapping sound drew my attention before I could check the notifications. My blood ran cold when I saw the ghost lounging against the stainless-steel refrigerator on the opposite side of the kitchen.

Dan followed my gaze to that spot, but his lack of reaction told me he didn't see the ghost.

I pointed anyway. "Our pirate ghost is back."

At my comment, the pirate strode toward me, his youthful face twisted in anger. "Why are ye interfering?"

"Why are you trying to hurt this family?" I fired back.

Dan's gaze swung back and forth between me and the empty space where he probably guessed the pirate ghost stood.

The ghost howled in response. His blue eyes flashed. "The boy should not have stolen me bottle. He brought this on himself."

"We tried to return the bottle," I countered.

"Consequences are consequences," he sang out.

"It's fine," I said with a calm I didn't feel. "Now that we know your name, Israel Hands, we can break the curse you placed."

Another howl reverberated, like it originated in my mind, and I clutched the sides of my head against the pain and intrusion.

"Sarah!" Dan cried out.

"What's happening?" Mandie yelled from the screen, now aiming up at the ceiling.

"Sorry, Mandie," Dan said, snatching his tablet back up and training it on me. "Sarah?"

I nodded at them both, the painful echoes of the pirate's howl fading. "I'm okay."

"'Tis what ye think," the pirate sang out again.

Dread snaked in my chest. "What does that mean?"

"You are sadly mistaken if ye think figuring out the name Israel Hands will solve your riddle."

The use of the word riddle threw me, but I focused on the first half of his statement. "You are Israel Hands?"

The pirate lifted his hands in a jaunty 'I don't know' gesture, causing the puffy long sleeves of his white shirt to slide down, revealing dirty but muscular forearms.

I snatched my laptop from the kitchen table and skimmed my latest notes. "Israel Hands, also known as Izzy, survived the final battle of Blackbeard, turned state's evidence like a petty little boy, and then fled to England like a coward, where he died a penniless beggar." My deliberate use of inflammatory language worked.

"I was not a petty lad or a coward," the ghost shouted, but his mouth thinned into an irritated line after.

"Thank you for confirming your name, Izzy," I said sweetly.

"Aye, fine, ye found me out." The pirate did a mocking version of a curtsy, one scuffed black boot in front of the other, legs bent awkwardly at the knees. "Though I always hated the nickname Izzy."

Bits of irritation buzzed around my mind. "What name did you prefer? Israel?" I asked, in part out of genuine curiosity, but also wondering if perhaps, we could convince the ghost to lift his curse. It was a long shot, but for the family, I had to try.

He sneered, lips curling above yellowed teeth. "Why

would I tell? And give ye more power than ye think ye have?"

Again, his odd word choice threw me, but before I could parse it further, he spoke.

"Basilica. Not that it'll do ye any good." He winked.

"Basilica," I repeated, noting that the name appeared in my notes, so at least somewhere in the reports of Blackbeard's crew, this was a real possibility.

"Aye?"

"What do you hope to gain from the curse?"

"Protecting the treasure for someone worthy," came his immediate reply.

"Jimmy told us you said that would one day be him. Is that true?"

"Maybe. I do not know yet."

Confusion washed over me and I pursued that emotion. "Are you sure that's the reason for the curse?"

"Of course 'tis!"

He sounded certain, but the confusion around me intensified and I began to doubt my questions. Ugh. That was his emotion clouding my mind. I strengthened my wall.

"Consequences are consequences," the pirate said, repeating his earlier refrain.

Before I could question or challenge that statement, he vanished from the kitchen and my mind felt fully my own again. "He's gone."

"What happened?" Dan asked, and I provided the ghost's side of the conversation to him and Mandie.

"Do you think he would have lifted the curse?" Mandie asked.

"No, I don't," I admitted, then remembered the second set of texts. A quick read of them before typing responses as I spoke to my team. "The family thanked me for whatever I had done because the intense anger they'd been experiencing retreated." I frowned. "Jimmy especially was hit hard by that round of the ghost's emotional presence."

"Now that we know that Israel 'Basilica' Hands is the ghost, we need to revisit Marie Lowell." The remaining reverberations of the ghost's influence on my mind still hurt, but I wasn't the one who found his bottle. The increased difficulties Jimmy was experiencing worried me. "We're running out of time."

CHAPTER FOURTEEN

"Thank you so much for seeing us again so soon," I said to Marie Lowell when she opened her front door.

"Of course, though I had not expected you to learn the name in less than an hour." She turned from the door, her long flowered dress swirling as she walked through her home toward the back room. We followed in silence.

Once in the back room, I startled when I saw the table tucked in the far corner already prepared for our latest attempt to break the curse.

I must have made a noise of surprise. "You haven't been away that long. I never cleared the table," Marie explained, before waving her hands over the two chairs on either side of the table.

Dan and I sat on either side of the wooden table and a strong sense of déjà vu swept over me. The black tapered candle remained in the middle, flanked on either side by the stoppered decanter of holy water and a cluster of mint leaves. I retrieved the cursed rum bottle from its plastic bag and set it on the table.

"What name do you have for me?" Marie asked.

"Israel Hands." I crossed my fingers under the table, hoping the bit of luck would bolster the curse-breaking.

Marie lit the black candle and held one of the mint leaves over it. As it burned and the sweet scent of mint filled the room, she spoke. "Israel Hands, you have made this cursed bottle. We banish your curse. Today, we claim a blessed cure for the Mackey family. We ask for a spiritual cleansing." As the candle continued to burn, she blew out the blackened mint leaves and dropped them in a small ceramic bowl. She pulled the stopper from the holy water and splashed some onto the liquor bottle, repeating the spell.

That dreaded sense of déjà vu strengthened when she frowned as she finished.

"No, not again," I cried, a sense of failure and despair flowing over and around me. Not all of that felt like my emotion and I wondered if it came from Marie or Dan.

Marie tilted her head in question.

"Okay, just like with Blackbeard, Israel went by other names." I bit my lower lip. "His nickname was Izzy—"

"But he didn't like that," Dan pointed out.

"True. We can try it anyway, but let's try Basilica Hands first."

Marie quirked an eyebrow.

"Israel Hands was Blackbeard's second in command," I explained. "He's explained that Blackbeard nicknamed him Izzy, but he never liked that name."

"He preferred Basilica?"

"That's what he said." I tapped my fingers on the tabletop. "He's a confused ghost, though, obsessed with a treasure that may or may not exist."

"Folks have been seeking Blackbeard's treasure for hundreds of years. This ghost says he knows where it is?" Marie asked with a snort.

"He does," I confirmed. "But, you know ghosts."

Marie chuckled. "I do. It's just as likely there was never any treasure and he's become lost, stuck on our plane."

"Exactly. He's been tied to this rum bottle hidden in a secret wall compartment since his death."

"Plenty of time for everything to warp."

"Yep." I frowned. "Except, he wouldn't have been confused before his death when he placed the curse."

The three of us sat in silence for a moment, considering the implications. I lifted a shoulder in a shrug. "All of that is purely academic. Right now, the main issue is freeing the Mackeys."

Marie placed either hand on the sides of her headwrap, as if to adjust the deep purple covering, but then laid her hands flat on the table instead. "Let's begin again, using the name Basilica."

The hairs on my arms rose in anticipation at the ghost's name. This was the right name. I knew it. Yet, fear and impending doom sizzled along my spine. Was that my emotion or something else? I focused on Marie's actions and words.

She broke off the burned tip of the black candle and emptied the ceramic bowl of the charred mint leaves. Muttering under her breath, she then relit the candle and repeated her steps. As the mint leaf burned again, she said, "Basilica Hands, you have made this cursed bottle. We banish your curse. Today, we claim a blessed cure for the Mackey family. We ask for a spiritual cleansing."

For a glorious half-second, I thought it worked. There was no crushing disappointment from Marie like before. The fear and impending doom vanished. Everything felt… back to normal.

Then the electric lights in the dimly lit room flickered.

"It worked. Until it didn't," Marie said, utter confusion in her voice.

A stench of decay clogged my nostrils, triggering my gag reflex.

Marie moaned. She leaned into the table, as if in physical pain.

"Sarah, what's happening?" Dan's worried question hung in the air.

"He's coming," I said in a robotic voice that barely resembled my own.

My mind swirled, the thoughts frenzied and the emotions feverish. I leaped from the chair, causing it to crash over backward. Dan and Marie startled at the clattering noise it made hitting the ground.

I held my hands out before me, as if that would stop a

spectral being bent on damage and destruction. This was it. I was going to die. It hardly seemed possible.

The air before me shimmered and the ghost I now knew to be Basilica Hands sparked into the visible realm.

"That was a good one," he said with a leer. "It gave me a good tingle."

"He's here," I said to the others before directing all my attention to the ghost. His angry yet gleeful energy—his signature—surrounded me, flowed over me, tried to slither into my mind. Thank goodness my protection wall held strong against the onslaught this time.

"Did ye think that would work?" he taunted me.

"You just said you could feel it," I challenged back, though it sounded weak even to my own ears.

His wide, snaggletoothed grin in response exposed the weakness.

"We'll just try again, with stronger words and talismans, Basilica," I said, desperation oozing from my voice now.

His eyes narrowed at my use of his name, but he swaggered toward me, his smell of mold and rotten flesh preceding him. "And ye will continue to fail."

"Why do I smell you?" I blurted out the question. Both Dan and Marie gasped at the question. Not a good sign, though one I couldn't pursue right at that moment.

"Perhaps because I smell so sweet." He blew a kiss at me and then drew a dagger from its sheath.

I took an involuntary step back and tried to calm my hammering heart. He couldn't hurt me with the weapon.

The ghost wasn't solid. A being without form could not cut me with an intangible knife.

But why could I smell him?

Instead of advancing toward me, Basilica flipped his grip on the knife so that it jutted to the side. He held it to his own throat and slid it across, in an obvious, crude, yet incredibly effective, threat directed at me.

"Is that a threat?" In part, I tried for false bravado, but also, I wanted to know if he was really threatening me.

"Why do ye ask questions ye already know the answers to?"

"Why are you doing this?"

"Why do ye ask questions ye already know the answers to?" he repeated, bored.

"There isn't even any treasure."

At my shouted statement, he paused and uncertainty shone in his eyes. As fast as it arrived, it left. Or his mad certainty pushed it out.

"We'll stop you." The tremor in my voice belied that statement, too, but I refused to cow before a demented pirate ghost who was haunting a family.

Basilica sheathed his dagger and jutted a hip my way. "No, ye will die."

Unfocused rage filled me and I grabbed the objects nearest to me. I flung the holy water at the ghost. It sailed right through his spectral image.

He belly laughed.

"Sarah, stop," Dan cried out, grabbing my arm.

I yanked myself free and, with a powerful fire burning

inside of me, grabbed the candle and chucked it after the holy water.

The ghost shook his head at my ineffectual actions.

My hands closed around the rum bottle and for a split second, fear flashed across the ghost's face. This was it. Now I would stop him. I pulled my arm back and with every ounce of strength I possessed, I hurled that dark bottle toward the infuriating ghost. He flinched as though it might hit him, but it sailed right through, just as the other objects did.

My shoulders slumped. However, I underestimated the strength behind that last throw, and the bottle didn't just fall harmlessly to the ground. It flew clear to the other side of the room and crashed into the opposite wall with such force that it cracked apart.

I covered my mouth with my hands in horror at what I'd done. The thickness of the rum bottle kept it from shattering, but the power of my throw had been sufficient to crack it apart. I rushed to the remnants, vaguely aware of Marie and Dan close at my heels.

The three of us stood around the large shards on the floor.

"Maybe we'll get lucky and that'll break the curse," I said into the shocked silence, my shaky voice eliciting slight chuckles from Dan and Marie.

"No, I don't think so," Marie said. "The spell did something. I'm just not sure what." Her earlier confusion coated her words.

"We'll check in with the family—" I stopped abruptly

and crouched. Beneath one of the large shards of dark glass appeared to be a slip of paper.

"What is that?" Dan asked, as my fingers closed around the paper, its subtle grid format creating a pleasant textural experience against my skin.

My first genuine smile since entering Marie's home bloomed as I read the inscription. "A clue."

CHAPTER FIFTEEN

"What does it say?" Dan asked, attempting to peek over the top of the scrap of paper. "Oh, that's some ancient writing."

"Yep," I agreed, squinting at the paper. "I don't think it'll be too difficult to figure it out. Honestly, it's all English." I offered a wide smile. "Right?"

Dan and Marie appeared less confident than I felt.

I ran my fingers around the paper. "Feels old. There are bumps; they feel like something within the paper itself."

"Do you think that's from pirate times?" Dan asked.

"Not sure," I answered with a shrug and skimming the half-sheet. "Oh, wait, there's a date at the bottom. 1755," I read. "And a name! Beatrice Knight."

"Beatrice Knight?" Dan repeated the name as a question. "Like the Knight House?"

"Probably." I returned to the beginning of the note. "Let me read this as written and let's see what we have."

Dan and Marie nodded their heads. Marie closed her eyes, perhaps to focus better on my words as I read.

I cleared my throat. "An you are reading this note, thee most likely wot thou art in grave danger. "

"That doesn't sound good," Dan interrupted.

"Mine own father became ill and bann'd this bottle. Unable to remove the ban, I placed mine own ban to break the ban and—"

"A ban?" That time, Marie was the one to interrupt.

"—hid the bottle in the mure to prevent this from betiding," I continued reading.

"That was a nice effort," Dan added.

"Y'all," I chastised them gently. "Let me get through it."

"Sorry," they murmured.

My reading continued. "That thou hast found this paper inside the bottle means I failed. But, fear not. Mine own ban shall allow thee to show that thou art worthy o' the treasure. This shall break the ban. Thee must solve the riddleth as written on each paper hidden in each location. For the first step, thou shalt begin at the end, in the shadow o' the final ward's sunrise corner. Thither thou shalt find the next riddle. Good luck, Beatrice Knight. Signed 1755."

The three of us stared in shock at each other. Dan broke the silence first.

"Solve the riddleth, I mean, riddles? We're going on a treasure hunt?"

Marie and I didn't miss the excitement in his voice.

"Yes," I said, "but keep in mind, this is to lift a curse. Not to find missing treasure."

"To-may-toe, to-mah-toe," he sang out, then sobered. "Of course, the primary focus is saving the family."

"Maybe not just the family," I mused.

"What do you mean?" Marie asked.

"Basilica Hands slashed at his throat, a clear sign of impending danger." I fluttered the paper I held. "And now, Beatrice Knight writes of grave danger and the necessity of completing her riddles to break the curse."

Marie paled at my words.

"What?" I asked, dread building.

"That is perhaps what I felt when you broke the bottle."

"What?" Dan repeated my question.

She dropped her gaze for a moment. "I would be willing to bet the curse now encompasses you, too."

"Me?" I squeaked the question.

"Sarah?" Dan questioned simultaneously.

"I fear so, yes," Marie confirmed her dire prediction.

"What do we do?" Dan asked.

"We solve the riddles." I ran my fingers over the textured paper again. "But first, we need a better sense of whether this paper is authentic. And we need to figure out the connection between Beatrice Knight and Basilica Hands."

Dan tilted his head. "We know from the historical record that Basilica Hands testified against Tobias Knight.

Could one of his descendants have done this to spite Hands?"

"Possible," I said, considering the likelihood. "Except Beatrice said her father became ill and placed the curse, but she dated her note 1755. Didn't Tobias Knight die in 1719, the year after his trial?"

Dan whipped his tablet out of his backpack and scanned his notes. "Yes. 1719." He counted aloud. "The time adds up for it to be a Knight child or grandchild. We don't have an age for his stepdaughter, but if she had a child within the next five years or so, her child would be an adult who could be Beatrice."

"So, her father could be an unnamed husband of Tobias Knight's stepdaughter." I shook my head. "That seems so convoluted for a Knight descendant to care that much."

Dan wiggled his eyebrows. "I mean, we are talking curses here. None of it is straightforward."

I laughed. "That's fair." An idea surfaced and I bit my lip, anticipating the likely reactions of Dan and Marie.

"What are you thinking?" Dan asked, his tone already exasperated.

"How do you do that?" I asked.

"What's your plan?" he said, instead of answering.

"I'm going to ask Basilica our questions."

Marie's jaw dropped open, but Dan just smirked. "That sounds about right," he said. "Just be careful."

"Always," I assured him. I concentrated on the letter and its connection to our ghost—or at least what we thought was a connection—and then directed my energy outward. "Basilica Hands? Are you here? I have a question for you." Despite my voice ringing out in confidence, a worm of disquiet wound its way up my spine.

Nothing happened.

I spun around, seeking that disturbance in the air that preceded his appearances. "Basilica? I want to ask you about Beatrice. Beatrice Knight. I believe you know her." That last stab in the dark, I hoped, would be enough to prompt the ghost.

With another half-turn, as anger surged in me, I gasped. "He's here." I spun again, finally sighting him near a shelf of amulets and candles.

"How dare ye summon me? With her name!" The ghost bristled with anger, one hand gripping the hilt of his dagger, though not drawing it from the sheath.

I held my hands up in faux-supplication. "We found a letter written by Beatrice Knight."

Confusion flittered across his rough features. "Letter?"

"Yes. In it, she mentions her father." A wave of indignation slammed into me. When I caught my breath, I realized we needed to stop. I faced Dan and Marie, lifting the letter and holding the edges, as if about to tear it. "What are we doing? None of this is our business. We need to leave well enough alone." My fingers tore the top.

"Stop!" Dan hollered at full volume.

My fingers stilled. Then tightened on the paper. The tear lengthened.

"It's the ghost's emotion. Stop what you are doing."

He grasped my hands with his, forcing my fingers to stop. "Listen to my voice," he said, now in a low, cajoling tone.

I shook my head twice, not saying no, but rather hoping the physical action would fling Basilica's emotions and desires from my mind. My brain frantically rebuilt my shattered wall of protection. The pirate ghost's energy was powerful.

"I'm okay now, thank you," I whispered to Dan, who released my hands, enabling me to set the paper on the table. I flexed my fingers to dissipate some of the tightness and give me a moment to think.

"Who is Beatrice Knight to you?" I asked the ghost, who glowered at me. He'd pummeled me with his emotion at the use of her name and the word father. "Are you her father?"

Instead of answering, he disappeared from our plane.

"He needs to stop doing that," I growled into the empty air.

"He left?" Dan asked.

"Yes."

"What do you think?" Dan asked.

"He seemed confused, but he sure reacted to my use of the word father in connection to Beatrice. Could he be her father?"

"If rumors of his death were greatly exaggerated," Dan quipped, "then the timing could work."

I pulled my cellphone from my jeans pocket. With a quick apology to Marie for throwing her things and making a mess, I placed the letter carefully on Marie's table and snapped a picture. Then I explained as I typed. "I'm sending the image to Mandie to investigate paper from mid-1700 to see if this seems consistent. Although it would be nice, I'm not as concerned with full confirmation of authenticity at this point." I hit send.

"While Mandie's researching that, we'll return to the rental to decode Beatrice's letter." I cradled the letter in the cupped palms of my hands. "Then we start our treasure hunt!"

CHAPTER SIXTEEN

Back in the rental, Dan and I were all set up at the kitchen table. My laptop was open, along with half a dozen documents and browser tabs. His tablet sat next to a pad of paper. Mandie was already live on video chat, though her head faced away, as she typed on her laptop off-screen. She was completing her research on Tobias Knight's family tree and the background of the paper from the rum bottle. Marie had excused herself from continuing along with us—after all, she had her own job to do—but she emphasized to call her if we needed her help.

"Let us know when you're ready," I said to Mandie, who nodded absentmindedly at me.

"One second," she said.

"How are the Mackeys doing?" Dan asked.

"Christine texted while we were driving to say they're

holding steady. Thankfully, nothing's worsening, but while I had my episode with Basilica at Marie's, they noticed an increase in their levels of anger. All of them. Not just Jimmy."

"That's not good," Dan said.

"No, it's not. And if I'm maybe going to start experiencing those symptoms, we need to decode this paper."

"I can shed some light on everything," Mandie said, chiming into our conversation.

"Please do," I said. "You have the floor."

She chuckled and shook her head at me, her brown curls bouncing. "The first part is easy. Based on your pictures of the note, and your description of the texture, I can reasonably conclude that it's made of what's called *laid* paper."

"Paper can get laid?" Dan asked, quirking an eyebrow at me.

"Behave, junior," I admonished, hiding a smile, although probably not too well.

Mandie continued as if neither Dan nor I had spoken. "Based on what I've found, laid paper was the most common until the mid-1750s, so that didn't change until after Beatrice wrote her note. It had a grid pattern, like the lines that you described, from actual wires in the material. If you hold it up to the light, you can see them."

I lifted the paper above our heads. Dan and I peered at it. Sure enough, you could faintly see the grid pattern. Mandie resumed after I returned the paper to the table.

"Based on the dated signature and the use of laid paper until that point, I'd guess it's from that time period. Of course," she cautioned, "it could be a forgery. But I don't know why someone would go to all the trouble to hide a fake paper in a rum bottle hidden in a wall."

"Unless they want to increase the tour value for the Knight House?" Dan asked.

"That's not unreasonable," I said, "but given how a teenager stumbled upon it, unlikely. Thanks, Mandie." I leaned toward the cellphone as if to disconnect the call.

"You don't think I'm finished, do you?"

I laughed and withdrew my hand. "My apologies. What else do you have?"

"There's definitely something fishy going on with the Knight family lineage."

"What do you mean?"

"We know Tobias died the year after his trial, and supposedly Basilica returned to England."

"Supposedly?" I prompted.

"Tobias's wife and stepdaughter never owned the Knight House, according to any historical documents I could find. It looks like an unknown Knight purchased the home with money from an unknown source."

"Any speculation at the time?" I asked.

"Much. The maybe-Knight that purchased the home went by the name Charles Tobias Knight. This intriguing combination set tongues wagging that he was an illegitimate child using some of definite-Knight's ill-gotten gains."

"Ooh, do tell," I said.

"When Tobias Knight, the original, married Catherine, already a widower, her deceased husband had borrowed a bunch of money from the church that he didn't pay back. Tobias refused to pay it either after marrying her, under the auspices of it not being his debt."

"The theory then was that he gave some of it to his illegitimate son before he died?" Dan asked.

"Bingo. There's zero proof of any of it, but that was the prevailing theory."

"How is Basilica Hands tied to that?" Dan asked.

"I'm guessing we think Charles Tobias Knight was Basilica Hands. That he used the name of the man he testified against because, I don't know, he thought it was funny. And he used some of Blackbeard's treasure to purchase the house," I answered for Mandie.

"Bingo, again," she said in response.

"That's a pretty solid theory." I started to end the call. "Anything else?"

"You need more," she said in mock-indignation.

I laughed. "Not at all. That was great. Thanks, Mandie!"

We ended the live video, and I faced Dan. "Now we need to decipher the note." I shifted the letter on the table between us. "Let's take this line by line."

"I'll start. 'An you are reading this note, thee most likely wot thou art in grave danger.' I don't know if I'm understanding every one of those words, but the threat seems clear," Dan said.

The image of Basilica's ghost slashing at his neck flashed in my mind. "I would agree with that assessment. What that will look like is uncertain. Perhaps hallucinations and emotional turmoil, like the family has been experiencing."

Dan rested his hand atop mine for a moment. "We'll solve this. None of ye are going to your graves." He ended his sentence with a pirate accent. The ploy worked, and I chuckled.

"The next line seems clear. 'Mine own father became ill and bann'd this bottle.' Since we know that there's a curse, it's reasonable to translate *ban* as *curse*," I said.

"Now that we believe Charles Tobias Knight and Basilica Hands are one and the same, that answers the question of how her father could have placed the curse," Dan continued. "Although, do we know if Charles Tobias Knight got married and had a child?"

I texted the question to Mandie. "We'll see what Mandie finds on that one."

"What about the part about her father becoming ill?" Dan asked.

"At this point, it may not matter, but in the interests of completeness, I'll have Mandie research that, too." I sent another quick text.

Dan continued reading. "The next line is 'Unable to remove the ban, I placed mine own ban to break the ban and hid the bottle in the mure to prevent this from betiding.' The only words I don't know are *mure* and *betiding,* though I can guess at them."

"Yeah, mure could be compartment, wall, or really anything like that. And, betiding sounds like something bad that she's trying to prevent. Especially since the next line is, 'That thou hast found this paper inside the bottle means I failed.' She thought that hiding it in the wall compartment would prevent anyone from finding the bottle and activating the curse."

"So then we get to her assurances," Dan said. "With her 'But, fear not. Mine own ban shall allow thee to show that thou art worthy o' the treasure. This shall break the ban.' Can I just say how much I love that this woman managed to place a counteracting curse? It's the ultimate, if you can't beat them, join them." Dan laughed at his own joke and I smiled wanly.

"And, the crux of the note: 'Thee must solve the riddleth as written on each paper hidden in each location. For the first step, thou shalt begin at the end, in the shadow o' the final ward's sunrise corner. Thither thou shalt find the next riddle.' The first line is again self-explanatory," I said. "The next part is the actual riddle."

Dan murmured the line under his breath and then shrugged. "I have no ideas. You?"

An idea had been percolating at the back of my mind. "Maybe." My fingers skimmed over the laptop's keyboard as I searched for the word *ward* on a site discussing the history of Savannah. A belly laugh erupted.

"What on earth could be that funny?" Dan asked.

"The word ward was used to describe Savannah's famous Squares," I explained. "Which means, Dan, that I was absolutely wrong in dismissing the Savannah Squares as important to the case."

Dan smirked in response before resuming our efforts to solve the riddle. "The line says 'begin at the end' and 'the final ward' – how many squares were there?"

"Over twenty," I answered, reading the open browser window before me. "At the maximum, there were 24, but a couple were lost, so now there are 22."

"Does it say which was the final square installed?"

I frowned, my eyes scanning the page, specifically the dates. "It does, but that was long after Beatrice wrote her note. It looks like the first six were installed between 1733 and 1742. Then there was a gap."

"The one in 1742 must be the final one."

"Yep. That's Upper New Square. Oh wait," I exclaimed. "Except it was renamed in 1787 after General James Oglethorpe, the founder of Georgia and the creator of the squares. So, it's Oglethorpe Square."

"Cool. We have a location," Dan said. "What about the end of the sentence, 'in the shadow o' the final ward's sunrise corner'?

"I suspect we'll need to be on site to figure that part of the riddle out," I said. "You didn't think it would be that easy, did you?"

CHAPTER SEVENTEEN

Our rental location continued to prove convenient. After grabbing a metal spaghetti spoon from the kitchen to use as a makeshift shovel if needed, Dan and I walked to Oglethorpe Square in ten minutes.

One of the more understated squares, with no monuments proclaiming anything, it had only a pedestal in honor of the Moravian missionaries who briefly called Savannah home. Benches ringed the square's brick sidewalk marking the square's boundaries. Like much of Savannah, immense trees overhung the small park, allowing the grass to stay green and dropping the midday temperature a tiny bit.

We sat on one of the wooden benches. Dan withdrew his tablet from his backpack and I opened my laptop. We didn't need Beatrice's riddle at this point. We'd both memorized it. But, we'd likely need to conduct some research.

"We're at the 'final ward', but what do we think 'in the shadow' of the 'sunrise corner' means?" Dan began.

Glancing around at all the trees, I speculated. "Perhaps the shadow refers to shadows provided by trees."

"Although hundreds of years ago, the trees wouldn't have looked like this."

"True." I typed on my laptop. "Let me see if I can find a sketch or drawing of the original Upper New Square."

"Too bad we're still decades before the invention of the photograph."

"Indeed." With a frown, I realized the futility of my task. "There's not much here, but nothing I'm finding looks anything like these towering trees. So, perhaps, something else caused the shadow in the riddle."

"What surrounded the squares back in the 1750s?"

I typed more, calling up a page I'd visited several times already. "According to this site, Savannah's 22 squares occupy a one-square-mile area of downtown, with each square about 200 feet north to south and 100 to 300 feet east to west."

We eyeballed the square in which we sat. Dan shrugged. "Sure, that could be accurate."

I laughed. "More importantly, it says that rows of homes and buildings for 'civic' usage originally surrounded the 'green space' squares."

"Could a building have created a shadow?"

"That seems the most reasonable. But, I wonder what

kind of paths were here then. They obviously didn't have this nice contemporary brick." I waved my hand to showcase the deep red brick before us.

"So maybe a home or civic building," Dan said. "Which corner do you think is the 'sunrise corner'?

I pulled up a current map on my cellphone. Twisting in my seat, I visualized the corners of the square. "We're bounded by State Street, Abercorn Street, and East York." I lifted my phone and tilted it to match the image on the screen. "It looks like maybe the square dips a bit on the Eastern side. So if the sun rises in the east, then the 'sunrise corner' must be the northeast corner of Abercorn and State." I squinted in that direction. "I think."

"Seems reasonable. Let's go see what's over there."

We gathered up our stuff and followed the brick sidewalk around to the corner, noting the famous Owens-Thomas house that confirmed our location.

"Trees. Trees. And more trees," I groused, wondering again why we were bothering. I sighed and plopped onto a bench. This was worse than looking for a needle in a haystack. "How on earth are we supposed to figure out what was around in 1755 when Beatrice wrote her childish riddles? I mean, come on. How is anyone going to be worthy of the treasure? They're just not." I leaned forward to place my elbows on my knees, ready to call it a day.

"Um, Sarah? Are you feeling alright?"

A hand stroked my upper back and some of the anger drained. I jumped to my feet, knocking Dan's hand off my back. I whirled around like a deranged lunatic, although at least with enough of my own emotions and control to not yell. "Basilica Hands, show yourself right now," I hissed.

Dan's eyes widened. "How is he here? We don't have the bottle with us. I thought it took longer for that to happen, like with the Mackeys."

"I don't know," I admitted, turning another half-circle. "It must be something about my clairempathy allowing him to latch onto me." I turned the rest of the way to face Dan.

A certain irritating pirate ghost lounged back on the bench, one booted leg crossed over the other, smirk firmly in place. "Ye rang?"

"How are you here messing with me?" My clipped voice dripped with irritation.

"Someone isn't feeling well on this early afternoon."

"Basilica. Honestly. What is wrong with you?" A growl erupted, eliciting a gasp from Dan and raucous laughter from the pirate. "Why couldn't you have gone into the light?"

"Uh, Sarah? Take a breath," Dan cautioned.

The pirate ghost quirked an eyebrow and stood to lean jauntily against a large oak tree. "How do ye know there's a light?"

I rolled my eyes and then tamped down the aggravation. None of this belonged to me. All of this anger and frustration—well, most of it—belonged to Basilica.

"What is going on here? You're new," came a soft voice. An older woman emerged from behind the tree Basilica leaned against. A wide-brim hat shaded her wrinkled face from the sun. A pale blouse tucked into what I believed to be britches, and a crocheted gray shawl covered her shoulders. Given the decades-old style clothing, I guessed reenactment actor. Until I saw she cast no shadow.

My eyes widened and Basilica bounced off the tree, whirling to face the new arrival. The three of us stared at each other for a beat, before all three started talking simultaneously.

"Who are you?" I asked.

"Blimey."

"You can see me!" Said the new ghost in an astonished declaration at me.

"Yes, I can. Who are you?" I repeated my question.

"Miss Margaret, though my friends call me Meta. I reside there," she said, gesturing toward the Owens-Thomas house. "Who are you?" she asked Basilica, who responded by leaving our plane.

I murmured to Dan, who stood next to the bench behind me, "Look up who haunts the Owens-Thomas house. Especially anyone named Margaret or Meta."

"Got it, boss," he replied, retaking his seat and typing on his tablet.

"I am quite confused, but this is very exciting. We rarely get livings who can see and interact with us." She frowned, her nose crinkling. "We're normally restricted to wasting energy with random noises. Although sometimes we can shriek." Her eyes danced mischievously. "Those are fun, though I often just wave."

I laughed. I liked this ghost.

"What are you doing here with the rude ghost?" she asked now.

"That's a long story," I said, before considering the ghost before me. It was a long shot that she'd know about anything buried, but why not? "Maybe you can help me."

"That sounds fun," she said, clapping her hands in excitement, albeit daintily.

I explained we were looking for something that could contain a riddle that would have been placed, probably underground, years before her time. "Not to be indelicate, but when did you pass?"

"1951. I was 80 years old."

A gasp sounded behind me, and I turned to Dan, who grinned from ear to ear. "I know who Meta is."

"Don't keep me in suspense," I whispered, keeping one eye on Meta, who frowned and rotated in a full circle, oblivious to our conversation about her.

"She was the final owner of the home. Margaret Gray Thomas, nickname Meta, was born and died there. She never had children, so she bequeathed the home and former slave quarters to Telfair Academy, which made it a museum. She waves to visitors from her gardens."

"That's so cool," I murmured, before returning my attention to Meta, who had finished considering the area of the surrounding square.

A smile illuminated her ethereal face. "I sense something beneath the surface."

"You do? How?" I asked.

"*Talking to the ghost?*" Dan mouthed at me, and I nodded.

"I am not entirely certain," she admitted in answer to my questions. "It gives off an unusual energy, which I have felt in this park before."

"Ooh, maybe the curse," I said.

"A cursed object would release energy," she concurred. "This way."

"We're following the ghost," I told Dan, who gathered up our things. He trailed me, following the ghost, to a spot beneath a large tree.

"Please don't be under this massive tree," I said as a quick prayer into the universe.

The ghost laughed, a sound like bells tinkling. "It is not. Rather, it is right here. Not too far below, I do not think."

"Thank goodness," I said, exhaling with relief. With a glance around, I was further relieved to realize that the tree before us and the shrubs behind us hid us from the view of passersby.

Dan held the metal spaghetti spoon aloft like a sword. "Tell me where I'm digging."

Meta pointed to the exact spot that, thankfully, was in the grass and not under a brick or a tree. I mimicked her pointing and Dan kneeled at the spot.

"About how far down does she say it is?"

The ghost answered his question, which I relayed to him. "She says it's not that far, maybe only a foot. It sounds like it might be another rum bottle."

Dan hacked at the grass, pulling it up in small clumps. He dragged the metal implement across the grass over and over. "I'm thinking maybe we visit a hardware store before the next riddle."

I chuckled. "That's fair." Then I kept watch while he dug, the hole becoming deeper and wider with his efforts. We continued to go unnoticed, and after some time, we heard a clank.

"I think this might be it," Dan said, setting the implement to his side, and using his hands to scoop out the last dirt obscuring the object. He pulled out the glass bottle and handed it to me. "Here you go. We found it."

I accepted the bottle, an exact match for the first one. Almost black glass; a wide, but squat height; and a medium-length neck. With a shake, I confirmed I could hear something moving around inside of it, also just like the first bottle. Excitement blossomed. "This is it. I'm sure of it." I faced the ghost. "Thank you so much for your help, Meta. We wouldn't have been able to do this without you."

"You are welcome. This is the most fun I have had in decades."

"We'll need to break the bottle to get at the paper. I'd rather not do that here and get glass everywhere," I told her ruefully. "We'll need to take this back to where we're staying."

Disappointment clouded her face for a moment, but then she beamed. "That is okay. Good luck on your journey."

"Thank you," I said again. She pulled her shawl tighter

across her narrow shoulders, then pivoted gracefully to walk toward the Owens-Thomas house.

"Let's head back to the rental," I said to Dan once she'd vanished from view.

"After we find a hardware store," he added.

CHAPTER EIGHTEEN

A quick rideshare back and forth to the nearest hardware store supplied us with a shovel, trowel, and pickaxe. We now stood in the backyard of our rental home. The latest rum bottle sat on a paver stone on the small patio. Dan and I eyed the bottle, uncertain.

"How do you suppose it remained undisturbed all this time, so relatively close to the surface?" Dan asked.

I frowned. "Not sure. Maybe something about the curse's energy protected it."

"Like your bubbles you encase invading energy in before releasing it?"

"Something like that," I answered, and we refocused on solving the issue of how to break the bottle.

"Should we just whack it with the pickaxe?" Dan asked.

I squatted next to the bottle. "I could just drop it like I did with the first one."

"That could work, too," he agreed, squatting beside me.

"Whatever makes the least amount of mess."

"The first one didn't shatter, so hopefully either method keeps the mess to a minimum."

"True." I leaned the bottle over on its side, considering the options. Whack it with the pickaxe or drop it. "Let's try the pickaxe. After all, when I broke the first one, I threw it at a wall. I'm not sure dropping would be enough force."

"Do you want the honor?"

"Sure, why not?" I agreed with a laugh, then stood to grab the pickaxe. I walked in a circle around the bottle, hefting the pickaxe. It was a cheaper one with a wooden handle, so a little heavier than the synthetic ones we'd seen at the store. I swung the pickaxe carefully, feeling it out. I'd want to use enough force to break the glass, without so much force to send glass pieces flying.

"Should I check online for the best method to do this?" Dan quipped.

I chuckled. "Smart aleck. I just don't want shattered glass going everywhere." I continued my evaluation of the bottle while Dan tapped on his cellphone. He scrolled through a couple of pages before stopping and reading.

"Huh, actually you're right. The side you use does make a difference in how it breaks. It sounds like the best option is to use the pointy side, as opposed to the axe side." He shrugged. "And then give it a whack."

"Let's see how it goes." As I lifted the pickaxe over my head, took a deep breath, and swung it down with what I hoped was a medium amount of force, a voice filled my mind.

"Yo-ho-ho, it's a pirate's life for you. Time to walk the plank." The voice slithered in my brain.

My aim thrown off, the spike scraped along the side of the bottle and cracked into the reddish-brown paver beneath. A chip of brick splintered.

"Does our security deposit cover that?" Dan joked, though I heard the worry even through my disorientation. "Are you okay?" he asked when I didn't respond to his joke.

"No," I whispered, my mind brimming with a gleeful pirate's voice chanting that I'd walk the plank. "Give me a second." I stared at the home's door, grounding myself in the present. No visual hallucination—or ghostly presence—accompanied the verbal assault, but I needed to shut that down.

"Time to walk the plank."

"Stop it," I muttered, squeezing my eyes shut. "Get out of my head."

"Time to walk the plank!"

I shook my head, as if that would remove the pirate's thoughts. Instead, they grew in intensity.

"TIME TO WALK THE PLANK! TIME TO WALK THE PLANK! TIME TO WALK THE PLANK!"

"Stop," I cried out, before clasping the sides of my head.

"Sarah, what can I do?" The question preceded Dan's

comforting hand on my back. He rubbed in circles when I didn't respond to his question.

"Get out of my head," I demanded in a harsh whisper. I focused on the pressure of Dan's hand on my back and the feel of the wind on my skin. Slowly, the screaming stopped and my mind was my own again. "Thank you," I told Dan as I turned to face him.

He wiped a tear from my cheek. The terrified expression on his face heightened my anxiety. "Do you need to strengthen your protection wall?"

I nodded, unable to speak further, instead focusing inward, placing stone after stone on my wall. An indeterminate amount of time passed, with me stacking the stones higher and higher. Dan stood beside me, a soothing presence.

A sigh escaped. "Okay, I think I'm good now."

"Was that Basilica?"

"I believe so." My eyes found the bottle on an adjacent paver, where it had spun from my first glancing blow. "Let's try again."

"You got this."

My foot moved the bottle back into the middle of the original paver. I lifted the pickaxe above my head again. My fear of the voice's return caused me to hesitate with bringing the pickaxe down. The bottle cracked upon the spike's lessened impact. Unfortunately, it left only a spike-sized hole but didn't break.

"Close," Dan said, encouraging me.

I pulled the spike out of the glass and lifted the pickaxe

over my head again. This time I swung with a bit more force, and was rewarded with a satisfying crack as the bottle split into several pieces.

"There it is," Dan whispered.

We stared at the slip of paper resting among the shards of glass. I brushed the glass aside and picked the paper up with the tips of two fingers. I shook it, just in case tiny glass shards remained, and brought it up to read. "This is definitely the second riddle."

Dan leaned over with the sweeper we'd brought out in preparation for breaking the glass. My phone ringing interrupted us.

"Hey Mandie," I answered.

He mouthed that he'd meet me inside. With a nod, I strode toward the door, ready to leave the anxious episode outside.

"What happened?" Mandie immediately responded.

"Of course, you can tell something happened."

"You sound off."

"I am," I agreed before bringing her up to speed, ending with the positive news that we had the second riddle. By that time, Dan had finished sweeping and joined me at the kitchen table. "Dan's here now, so I'm putting you on speaker."

"Hey Dan," she greeted him, which he echoed. "I've got news."

"We figured," I said.

"In the first riddle, Beatrice wrote that her father became ill, and that triggered him placing the curse, right?"

"Correct," I concurred.

"Based on information I found, Charles Tobias Knight, suspected alias of Basilica Israel Hands, married a woman named Eleanor in 1721—"

"The year after he bought the Knight House?" I asked.

"Yes. They had a daughter, Beatrice, the next year. Then came the good stuff," she dramatized. "The first yellow fever outbreak in Savannah happened in 1733, and as best I can tell, that's the year Charles Tobias Knight died."

I did some quick math in my head. "That would have made Beatrice about 12 years old?"

"Correct," Mandie said. "If her father placed the curse before he died, the early stages of delirium from yellow fever could be the cause."

"That makes sense," Dan said. "He still would have been able to function, but he wouldn't have been thinking clearly."

"And his widow and daughter might not have known anything about it at the time," I added.

"Even if he'd said something to one or both of them, they most likely would have dismissed it as the ravings of a demented, sick man," Mandie finished.

"When Beatrice found the evidence as an adult, she figured out what her father had done," I continued working through our information, "realized she couldn't simply undo his actions, so she placed the counter-curse."

"Smart woman," Dan said.

"Well, let's see if we can prove that we're worthy," I

quipped, using the pirate ghost's language. "We have the second riddle." I smoothed the paper flat on the table and read it aloud.

"Huzza, thou hast made it to the second riddle. Thou art one step closer to breaking the ban. The next one shall not be as easy. For the second riddle, thou shalt need to first find our namesake ward. Then, once at the ward, the next riddle is to be found withal unexpected ancestors. Seek Mico, our great friend. But, not too close! Respect above all else is crucial to discovery."

"That one seems mostly straightforward," Mandie commented.

"At least the early modern English is closer this time," Dan agreed.

"Except that Beatrice says this one won't be as easy as the first," I warned my eager colleagues.

"True," Dan said, peering over at the note. "The first thing would be to figure out what she means by 'our namesake ward'."

"Namesake has many meanings," Mandie said. "That could reference her family, the Knights."

"Or her original namesake family, Basilica Hands' birth name family," Dan added.

"But would a ward—one of the squares, that is—be named after either of those families?" I asked.

"Good point," Dan said. "It wouldn't."

"So 'namesake' must reference something bigger than her immediate family," Mandie continued our train of thought.

"I wouldn't think it would be too much bigger than the county, city, or state equivalent," I surmised.

"Yeah, I don't think anything would have been named after the colonies as a whole," Dan said.

"Is there a Savannah Square?" I asked aloud while I searched the internet for the answer. "Of course, it could only be one of the first six," I mumbled, as I narrowed my search. Out of the corner of my eye, I saw Dan searching on his tablet, and made the reasonable guess that Mandie was searching too. Between the three of us, we could figure this out.

"Found it," Dan said. "At least I think so."

"Which one is it?" I asked.

"Wright Square was originally named Percival Square when the city installed it as the second Savannah Square. And who was Percival?"

"Who was Percival?" I played along.

"John Percival is the gentleman who is largely credited with giving the colony of Georgia its name."

"That would fit the definition of namesake," I said. "Good work, Dan."

"Thanks, boss."

I reread the riddle. "The next line is about finding the riddle 'withal unexpected ancestors'. What do we think that means?"

"I can answer that," Mandie's voice popped in. "I just searched for 'Mico Percival Savannah Square' and a page on the Georgia Historical Society provided the answer."

"That would be?" I prompted.

"The unexpected ancestors are probably the Native Americans, given that they haven't always been considered connected to white people."

"That makes sense," I agreed.

"Mico turns out to be the nickname for the Yamacraw Chief Tomo-Chi-Chi, who was instrumental in the safe founding of Savannah. After his death in 1739, he was buried in Percival Square, since renamed Wright Square. Unfortunately," she continued, "his original grave was in the middle of the square, which is problematic enough. But, 100 years later, the grave was desecrated, and the bones scattered, to make way for a new memorial for someone else."

"Ouch, harsh, and totally disrespectful," Dan said.

"For sure," I agreed. "But in terms of our search, that might be okay."

"What do you mean?" Mandie asked.

"Beatrice's riddle says to not get too close because respect is crucial to discovery. In her time, the grave wasn't desecrated. She wouldn't have wanted to do that either."

"The next liquor bottle containing a riddle might not be very close to the original gravesite," Dan concluded.

"Exactly." I furrowed my brow. "On the other hand, I'm not sure how else to find where she buried the third riddle. Near, but not too near, the original grave, in the middle of the square, is still a pretty wide area."

"And pretty wide open to people seeing us," Dan added.

I grinned. "Guess it's time to visit Wright Square."

CHAPTER NINETEEN

The close proximity of the original squares to our rental—and each other—remained a blessing. We made quick work of the walk to the second square in our quest to break the pirate's curse. The crowds had grown, as it was now approaching the end of the workday for many people.

Wright Square, on the surface, looked remarkably like Oglethorpe Square, with towering trees, winding brick pathways, and benches to enjoy the tranquility. However, unlike the first square we visited, this one had a soaring monument at its center. When we reached it, a marker stood to tell us what we were looking at. Except that wasn't quite right. The small marker on a single pole in the ground didn't describe the monument behind it.

"Oh, so this is where Tomochichi's grave and original marker had been," Dan said in a hushed voice. The soaring monument was actually for William Washington Gordon, a railroad pioneer for the state.

"Good for him, but not cool to Chief Tomochichi," I said, then spun around. I pointed toward the southeast corner of Bull Street and York Street. "Didn't the website say the replacement Tomochichi's monument is on Bull Street?" We hustled over to a large granite boulder. A bronze tablet encircled with roses and arrowheads was inscribed with 'In memory of Tomochichi – the Mico of the Yamacraws – the companion of Oglethorpe – and the friend and ally of the Colony of Georgia.'

"Although, hold on a second," Dan said, placing his hand on my arm. "The chief's original grave wasn't yet desecrated in Beatrice's time, remember? Maybe we need to start our search back at the Gordon monument." He gestured back toward the central stone pillar.

"True, but the website said the ghost of Tomochichi haunts the square at his current monument."

"What's your plan?"

"The ghost hunter page says to walk around the new monument three times and the ghost of Tomochichi might appear."

"And you want to do that why?"

"I'm hoping he might help us narrow down the search, the way Meta did," I said excitedly. If I was going to be super-in-touch with ghosts while in Savannah, I might as well get the most possible benefit out of it.

Dan and I eyed the monument. "Do you think you need to walk clockwise or counterclockwise?" he asked.

"There's no need to do all that," a voice said dryly from behind me.

When I turned, a Native American stood behind us. I doubted he was from my century, based on his clothing. He wore what appeared to be a tanned buckskin draped over his bare shoulders, and a breechcloth over leather leggings. A kerchief of sorts wrapped around his neck. The deep wrinkles across his face suggested this may have been how he looked toward the end of his long years.

I stumbled a moment before responding to his comment. "You speak English?"

"I do, now. In my time, we had an interpreter. After a couple hundred years, you learn new things," he explained.

I gaped at him. "That's awesome."

Dan looked in the direction I did and, even though I knew he couldn't see the ghost, he waved. "It's an honor to meet you, Chief Tomochichi."

"Thank your young fellow for me," the chief responded, and I did. "Now, what can I help you with? It's not every day that the living can see more than my ghostly image."

He said this last with a touch of ruefulness and my heart broke, as always, for ghosts who didn't move on.

"Don't be sad for me, miss," the ghost chided with a half-smile. "I could move on if I wanted. I'm not stuck here because of that—" He gestured toward the monument in the center of the square that supplanted his grave. "—but because I choose to stay. Even if it is sometimes bittersweet."

"Why do you choose to stay?" I impulsively asked.

"The world's changes keep me intrigued."

"I can only imagine how amazing it is to see those changes," I marveled.

"You have no idea."

"To answer your question," I said, getting down to business, "we're trying to undo a curse." He quirked an eyebrow at that before I explained what we were trying to do and how Meta had helped us before.

"Fascinating." He glanced around the square. "That sounds like something I should be able to do as well."

"We would be so appreciative. This family…" I trailed off with a shake of my head. Not just the family. I was in danger, too. No long-term good could come from being this in touch with the ghostly realm, I knew. Not to mention the pirate's tormenting of me at his whim now.

Chief Tomochichi began to walk across grass, brick, and dirt. We scrambled to follow. He glanced around as he did so, in the trees, through the shrubs, and at the ground. Just as I worried we wouldn't find the bottle's location, the chief halted.

"Here," he said, pointing at the base of a shrub.

I sighed. It was practically on top of the Tomochichi historical marker. I pointed it out for Dan's benefit.

"That's gonna be a rough one," he commented, as we both observed how much busier this square was than the one we visited earlier.

The chief picked up on our unease. "If it was easy, I suppose it would not break the curse."

I chuckled and some of my tension released. "You are correct. We'll make it work."

"Somehow," Dan inserted, lips thinned in thought.

"Thank you so much, Chief, for your help. I'm glad to hear that you're staying on our plane because you want to, and I hope you continue to enjoy the passage of time." I opened my mouth to ask another question, then thought it impertinent and closed my mouth.

"Ask your question, young lady."

"Do you think you'll ever cross over?"

He appeared thoughtful. "One day. That day is not today. Good luck on your quest." He strode away.

I called out goodbye as he vanished from my sight. "What do you think?" I asked Dan.

"I think we're going to have to pretend we're doing something official."

"Like what?"

Dan rummaged in his backpack for a moment and withdrew a clipboard. He clipped a piece of paper with columns on it. "Don't let anyone get too close, though," he said, showing me the details. "I was helping my niece with her astronomy assignment. Not too relevant in an Earth park."

I laughed. "You at least look like a supervisor." He indeed looked the part in his ironed dark brown polo shirt and khaki shorts.

He faced away from me, holding the clipboard at chest height and then frowning at it as if working. "Don't waste my valuable time," he said with faux brusqueness.

"Got it, boss," I said with a mock salute, not missing the corner of his mouth rise. Then I kneeled in the dirt to dig the grass up with the trowel. At least it was next to just this simple pole, and not under the actual monument. With the first strike of the implement on the ground, a high-pitched squeal sounded. I sat back on my heels and looked around. "Did you hear that?"

"Hear what?" Dan asked.

I didn't answer, but struck the ground a second time. The screech sounded again. I dropped the trowel and gripped the sides of my head. "You really don't hear that screech?"

Dan faced me, worry etched across his face. "What's happening? I don't hear anything. Is it a ghost?"

"I don't know," I said, uncertain what to do. Part of me hesitated to strike the ground a third time. The piercing noise was that horrific. The larger part of me, though, knew I needed to continue.

Bracing myself for the sound, I hit the ground and pulled the trowel through the grass and dirt, the appalling noise echoing throughout my mind. The closest thing I could approximate it to was the sound of a hundred fingernails dragged down a hundred blackboards. I wondered how long before my ears bled from the assault. Tears formed and leaked out the corners of my eyes.

"Are you crying?" Dan squatted beside me, hand on my back. "What's happening?"

"I don't know." Helplessness engulfed me. "Maybe you should try digging and I—"

"Excuse me," came a curious voice from above us. "What are the two of you doing?"

I swiped a hand across my cheek to erase the tears before Dan and I rose to face the owner of the voice.

Oh no, exactly what we feared. Someone official had taken notice. Except, she was wearing jeans and a t-shirt. Not quite official park service clothing.

"We're on official business," Dan said officiously, waving the clipboard with the astronomy assignment clipped to it.

"I work this area for Park & Tree, and I don't recognize you," the woman responded, her tone suspicious.

A vague recollection that Park & Tree were the park service workers hit me and I groaned.

"Are you okay?" she asked me. Her brown eyes narrowed. "Have you been crying?"

Guess I hadn't wiped my tears well enough. "I may have hit my finger with this." I showed her the trowel.

She took in Dan's attire, her brown eyes inquisitive. "Why don't you have your uniforms? Are you new?"

"Yes," Dan answered, apparently deciding to roll with whatever assumption the lovely woman made. He stepped closer and gave an impish smile. "I'm Dan. This is Sarah."

YO-HO-HO. I winced at the voice in my head, attempting to turn away from Dan and the actual official, keeping them only in my peripheral vision. Dan caught my movement and also turned to try to block me from her.

"What's your name?" he asked her. Even in my distress, I noticed the flirtatious tone.

She ran a hand through her blond hair. "I'm Tessa. When were you hired?"

Dan leaned closer to her. "Can I tell you a secret, Tessa?"

"Of course," she said, matching his movement.

"We don't work for Park & Tree," he admitted.

"Yeah, I know," she said with a smirk. "I was curious how far you'd take this."

YO-HO-HO, IT'S A PIRATE'S LIFE FOR YOU. UNTIL YOU DIE.

Dan offered a version of what we were doing. In between bouts of the pirate shrieking in my ear, I heard a handful of words and phrases. It was all I could do to remain on my feet, swaying from the impact of each scream.

"—geocaching—" from Dan.

WALK THE PLANK!

"—you can't really—" from Tessa.

I'M GIVING YE NO QUARTER.

"—promise to put everything back—" from Dan.

DEAD MEN TELL NO TALES!

"—I don't know—" from Tessa.

YE LILY-LIVERED LANDLUBBER.

I squeezed my eyes closed against the onslaught and swore at Basilica to GET OUT OF MY HEAD.

His ghostly laughter met my demand.

You won't stop us, I assured him.

Maybe not today. But I will.

The tension in my brain decreased, and I heard the end of Dan and Tessa's conversation.

"Okay," Tessa said with a giggle.

"Thank you so much," Dan said. "We appreciate it. It shouldn't be that deep. As soon as we find the bottle, we'll refill the hole. You'll never know we were here."

"I just don't know."

"We'd never get you in trouble. I promise."

My exhausted brain thought to itself, *Dan's as sweet as a Georgia peach.* What the—? I fanned myself with my shirt and considered my state of disarray. The sweat was entirely because of the internal battle with the pirate and had nothing to do with Dan.

"Just try to finish quickly," Tessa said, decision apparently made.

"Will do."

"Good luck." Tessa waved over her shoulder as she walked away.

"Thank you," Dan called after. As soon as she was out of earshot, he spun to me. "What happened? Are you okay?"

"I'm okay now," I said, voice shaky. I explained what I'd heard. "Let's just get this bottle and get back to the rental before he tries again."

Without a word, he pried my fingers off the trowel and kneeled on the ground to pick up where I'd left off.

I massaged the feeling back into my fingers; I'd had no idea I'd been gripping it so tightly.

Dan scraped away the dirt. Soon we heard the clank that let us know we'd hit pay dirt. So to speak.

Dan used his fingers to wipe away the last of the dirt covering the rum bottle and then lifted it from its home for the past hundreds of years. He looked up at me. "The third riddle. Let's get it to the house and see what it has to say."

CHAPTER TWENTY

By the time Dan and I reached the rental, I almost felt normal again. The copious amount of sweat hadn't dried because of the humidity, but at least it wasn't still pouring off of me. My head still pounded with a dull ache, and my muscles begged me to take a nap. Although a cup of coffee would help me buoy myself, our first step was breaking the newest rum bottle. We had a riddle to solve.

We dumped our backpacks on the kitchen table and then retreated out to the paver deck. I placed the squat, dark bottle on the same paver we'd used before. The small splintered spot was visible. Knowing my debilitated state, Dan stepped up to crack the bottle. I sat a safe distance away, although based on our experience before, it seemed unlikely for any glass shards to go flying.

Sure enough, Dan swung the pointed end of the

pickaxe at the bottle, and with a single controlled swing, cracked it on the first try.

"Very nice," I said, clapping my hands.

He leaned over to retrieve the slip of paper and handed it to me. "Please, do the honors."

I cleared my throat and read Beatrice's third riddle. "How wonderful, thou hast solved the second riddle. The next step in proving thy worth shall be found in the center o' the beginning. Not sure what I mean? Advise the origins o' our great city, and one o' the men responsible. Hither thou shalt find the third riddle in thy assay to break the ban."

"Okay, that sounds fun. Assuming it's another ward— I mean, square—let's get to translating," Dan said.

Together, we traipsed back into the house. Dan made coffee while I set my laptop and his tablet at what had become our usual side-by-side seats. I placed the riddle on the wooden table between our two places.

The aroma of medium roast brew soon filled the space. I inhaled deeply, already experiencing the relaxing yet invigorating influence of the smell.

Dan carried two mugs of coffee to the table and we both sipped at the deliciousness. Then we got to work.

"The first line is a gimme, of course," I said. "Though I appreciate her ongoing support."

"She seems like a nice lady," Dan agreed. "The second line starts easy enough. We know we need to prove our worth to break the curse. But what do we think 'in the center of the beginning' means?"

"Going with your assumption—which I agree with—that these riddles will refer to one of the six wards in existence at the time of her notes, the beginning is either the first square or the middle of the original squares. Is there another meaning I'm missing?"

"Well, if it's the middle of the original squares, that opens two possibilities. The first four. Or the six at the time of her writing."

"Good point. I'd think she'd mean the first four, since the next two were installed a few years later." I read the next line silently. "She expected the riddle-solver to face multiple options."

Dan laughed. "True. 'Not sure what I mean?' is pretty clear-cut."

"But how does the next line help? 'Advise the origins o' our great city.' That doesn't narrow it between our options, I don't think." I furrowed my brows in concentration. "Advise doesn't sound like it's being used the way we would today."

"I agree it doesn't. If we let that go for now, and focus on the part of the sentence after the comma, maybe that will shed light on the beginning part."

"Okay, so she says 'one o' the men responsible' to complete that sentence. 'Advise the origins o' our great city, and one o' the men responsible.' Who are the men responsible for the city of Savannah?"

Dan typed on his tablet. "We already discovered Oglethorpe as the primary architect." He frowned. "Hmm, everything that's coming up is either Oglethorpe or

Tomochichi. Oh, wait, Mary Musgrove is also mentioned."

"I recognize that name. Who is she?"

More typing from Dan. He whistled. "Cool, she was the interpreter that Tomochichi mentioned."

"Ah, right, but it doesn't help us, since the riddle specifies it's a man."

Silence descended on the kitchen as we typed furiously, putting in every combination of words and questions we could think of to identify another man who shared responsibility with Oglethorpe and Tomochichi in the founding of Savannah.

And then I metaphorically smacked my forehead. "We're going about this the wrong way."

"We are?"

"Yes. We're confident the third riddle is located in one of the original four or six Savannah squares." My voice rose in my excitement and I scanned my notes for the right link. "Let me find the page we were on before. The squares are named after various bigwigs. I can look for the square that mentions someone involved in the founding." I slapped the tabletop. "There he is. Robert Johnson, colonial governor of South Carolina."

"I don't understand. What does he have to do with Savannah?"

"He's credited with helping Oglethorpe grow the colony of Georgia, which was really just Savannah. Johnson Square was the very first square installed."

"Ooh, that was a tricky one."

"Indeed. Which is why Beatrice had to give us two hints."

"She's very helpful like that, Miss Beatrice."

"She is," I agreed. "We're not finished yet."

"Let's get to it."

"I believe the next riddle is in the middle of Johnson Square. That seems to be what the last line, 'Hither thou shalt find the third riddle in thy assay to break the ban', is saying.

"Assay?"

"Not entirely certain, but maybe something like search, attempt, or quest."

"I like quest," Dan said, "so we'll go with that."

"Although it doesn't fit the sentence," I pointed out. "I agree it's cool, however."

"What's our final translation?"

I typed several careful notes into my open document before responding. "Our best guess: 'How wonderful, you have solved the second riddle. The next step in proving your worth will be found in the center of the beginning. Not sure what I mean? Consider the origins of our great city, and one of the men responsible. Here you will find the third riddle in your attempt to break the curse.' What do you think?"

"I think it's time to continue our quest in the center of Johnson Square," Dan responded with two thumbs up.

CHAPTER TWENTY-ONE

"I'll bet we could do this in our sleep," Dan joked while we made our way to Johnson Square in the waning light. As we passed sights and sounds that were becoming increasingly familiar, I couldn't help but agree with him.

"We're here," I said when we reached the northwest corner of the square at Bull and Bryan Streets. "We know we're going to the middle." From our research, we knew this largest of the squares contained an obelisk monument, two fountains, and even a sundial. Naturally, the square was like its fellow brethren, filled with red brick walkways, towering trees, and the occasional wooden bench.

Of course, the obelisk sat in the center of the square. We stared up at it, considering our options. "This didn't exist in Beatrice's time," I said, biting my lower lip. The stone monument had a large square base. Short shrubs surrounded the foundation, and then another larger area of ground covering surrounded that.

"Good thing you can ask one of your friends to help us," Dan mumbled out of the corner of his mouth, in imitation gangster-style. "Are any of them present?"

Not only were no ghosts present, but my mind was blessedly free of all outside emotions. My wall of protection was doing a fantastic job keeping everyone in the square out, as well as Basilica, at least at that moment. Unfortunately, we needed a ghost. There was zero chance we'd identify where Beatrice might have hidden a rum bottle years before the monument was a glimmer in someone's eye.

"Let's run through the usual suspects for this square," Dan said, pulling his cellphone out of the pocket of his khaki shorts. He typed and scrolled as he spoke. "We know this is the Nathanael Greene Monument, named after the Revolutionary War hero. Huh, he has his own square. It looks like his bones were lost for a time, but then he was interred here. His son later died in the Savannah River, and his bones are here too." He scrolled more. "The sundial is dedicated to Colonel William Bell—"

"Wait a minute," I interrupted him. "Are there any stories of ghosts known to haunt this square? That's who helped us before."

"Good point," Dan said, immediately calling up a page about hauntings at Johnson Square. "I'm not finding much."

"I'm surprised by that," I said. "In a city as haunted as

Savannah, there are no known hauntings of Johnson Square?"

"That's not quite what I said."

I considered rolling my eyes but decided that would be childish. "What did you find?"

"A six-year-old who died in 1889. Little Gracie."

"Oh." That was indeed not much. Savannah's ghosts had a lot of experience and, for them, interaction with the living. Many of them had held onto their sanity. But, a young child who died over one hundred years ago? "That's it?"

"Sorry, boss. Not only that. She played in Johnson Square outside of her parents' hotel. Although she greeted guests there, and was apparently sweet and adorable, her ghost haunts Bonaventure Cemetery where she's buried. People report the marble statue her father commissioned for her grave walks around at night." He replaced his cellphone in his pocket. "What's the play?"

"I'm going to try to contact Gracie. Maybe that's why I don't feel her here. But she's tied to this place, too, so..." I lifted my hands, palms up, in a shrug. "It's the only play I see. We can't start digging around the monument without any kind of plan. And, I'm not sure all the luck in the world will help if the riddle is underneath the center of the monument."

"Very true." He laced his fingers in front of him. "Let me know if I can do anything."

"Thanks." Closing my eyes, I allowed my arms to hang loosely at my sides. I removed a single stone from my wall of protection. Then another. And another. But felt nothing. No supernatural energy at all. In a city as haunted as Savannah? That seemed preposterous.

Gracie Watson? Are you there?

No response from anything or anyone. A tendril of anxiety snaked around my core. There was no way that *nothing* supernatural was here.

Is anyone here? I'm looking for Gracie Watson. Does anyone know her?

No response again. Nothing supernatural pushed at my mind, tried to slither in. It was a flat, energy-less white nothing.

Is anybody there? Anyone who can communicate with me?

"Yo-ho-ho, I'm here," came a snarky voice not inside my head.

My eyes flew open, and I gasped. Basilica leaned against the base of the monument, his scuffed black boots barely visible through the shrubs he stood in.

"I'm the only one who can communicate with you."

"You know that isn't true," I reminded him. Out of my peripheral vision, I saw Dan startle at my comment and ease closer to me.

"It is now," the pirate snarled.

The hair on my arms rose at his ominous words. "What does that mean?"

Basilica pushed off the monument and sauntered over the grass, stopping less than a foot from me. This close, I smelled the rotten seawater emanating from his form. I restrained myself from flinching or stepping backward. "Why do ye think none of the ghosts are talking to ye? Do ye think your protections are that powerful?" He sneered at the word *protections*.

I swallowed past the lump in my throat, an action that did not go unnoticed by my ghost visitor.

"Ye did, I see." He laughed, a deep, phlegmy bark of a laugh. "That was a mistake."

Motion behind Basilica, on the left side of the monument, drew my attention. Someone was peeking out from around the bottom left edge of the monument. Someone who appeared young. And made of marble.

"What?" The pirate ghost whipped his head around to look in the direction of my gaze. But the person I'd spotted had vanished.

"Nothing," I lied. "Why don't you just leave?"

"Why don't you?"

Instead of answering, I stepped past him, ignoring my strong desire to recoil at being near the ghost. "I'm going to replace the stone in my wall of protection, and we'll see who is more powerful. I predict you'll vanish." My voice remained steady, even though I was hyperventilating inside.

"I grow bored with these games."

I didn't have to turn to know that Basilica had left the square. My mind cleared. "You can come out now," I said, my voice soft and low, directed at the monument.

"What's happening?" Dan whispered.

"Basilica was here, causing trouble. He's gone now." I

dropped my voice more. "I think I saw Gracie. That's who I'm trying to coax out now."

"Understood." Dan stepped out of even my peripheral vision.

I directed all of my energy and understanding forward. "Gracie? Is that you?"

The marble head poked around the base of the monument. Then a young child made of marble revealed herself. She walked stiffly toward me, though the marble moved in unnatural ways, rolling as if not solid. The marble ghost stopped ten feet from me, eyeing me warily.

"Are you Gracie?"

"How do you know me?" she asked in response, her sweet, calm voice in opposition to the repetitive movement of running her hands up and down the sides of her dress. Big eyes opened wider under a thick fringe of bangs. Her long hair curled past her shoulders in marble waves. She was the most interesting ghost I'd ever seen.

"I don't," I admitted.

"Why did you call me?" she asked. She offered a tentative smile.

I kneeled at her height, aware that I looked like I was talking to the air.

She closed the distance between us.

"I need your help, Gracie."

"What about the bad man?" She wrinkled her nose in disgust, leaving me to wonder if she could smell him, too.

"He's gone now. He can't hurt you." I hoped that part was true.

"How can I help you?"

It made sense why people liked her when was alive. She didn't know me, yet was curious about me and wanted to help a stranger. "We're looking for a bottle."

"A bottle?" She frowned in confusion. "Where?"

"That's what we need your help with." I pulled out my cellphone. She reached out a marble hand, not quite touching the device.

"I have seen that toy," she said with a tinkling little girl laugh.

"It's more for adults," I explained, and she nodded in understanding. She seemed childlike, but more developed than six. I wondered if it was like the chief, who learned English while a ghost. Perhaps Gracie 'grew' in her own way as a ghost. I focused on the task before me, scrolling through the pictures on my phone until I found one of the original cursed bottle. I showed her the image. "Do you see that bottle?"

She nodded.

"Somewhere near this—" I indicated the monument behind her. "—buried in the ground is a bottle that looks like this." We were screwed if it wasn't in a bottle like this. "Because of the curse surrounding these objects, other ghosts have been able to direct their energy at the ground and see what's below. Does that make sense? Do you think you can find it?"

She frowned again, though more in deep thought than distress. Her face cleared, and she offered a wide grin. "Yes." Gracie faced the monument. From behind her, I watched as she rotated her head from the left to the right and back again. I assumed she was methodically checking the ground for our hidden bottle.

Just as I despaired this search would be a bust, she spun around, the bottom of her mid-calf marble dress flaring. "I found it."

"Where is it?" I asked, my eyes wandering like I could see beneath the surface to identify the location without her.

Gracie turned back toward the monument and extended her right hand, pointing her index finger to the right edge of the monument.

I sighed in relief. The bottle wasn't underneath the monument. One crisis averted.

The little marble ghost walked over to the monument and then sat cross-legged on the ground. She leaned over to touch a spot about a foot from her. "Here."

I gestured at Dan to follow me. "This is my friend, Dan. He's going to help me get the bottle out of the ground."

Gracie nodded her marble head.

With our prior practice, Dan made short work of breaking ground and using the trowel to uncover the rum bottle. It matched its earlier mates.

Thankful for the shrubs providing a bit of protection on this side of the monument, I watched Dan refill the hole. It was obvious the ground had been disturbed. In the morning, maybe the park workers would assume an animal did it overnight. Dan placed the bottle in his backpack and slung the bag over his shoulder.

"I helped?" Gracie asked, her little girl voice at odds with the marble appearance.

"You did, Gracie." I wanted to hug her but thought better of it. She wasn't corporeal, despite the fantastical stories of her actual marble statue walking around the cemetery. I'd fall through her and hit the ground.

Without another word, but with a huge smile on her face, Gracie walked back behind the monument, and presumably returned to the Bonaventure Cemetery.

I joined Dan on the brick walkway. "If there's one riddle for each of the original six Savannah squares, we've only just now passed the halfway mark. It's just about nighttime. We need to pick up the pace before Basilica finds a more successful way to interfere." I filled Dan in on Basilica's attempts to thwart my communication with the ghosts.

"Let's get this bottle back to the rental."

CHAPTER TWENTY-TWO

We'd become experts at breaking the bottles, so Dan made quick work of this one, and within minutes we perched on our seats at the kitchen table. Except, instead of being elated at finding the message, we were confused.

The slip of paper from inside the bottle sat on the table. We'd already read it several times. I reread it again.

"Huzza! Well done on finding the final riddle. Thou hast almost proven yourselveth worthy enough to break the pirate's ban. As 'tis the final riddle, this one shall not be so easy as the others have been. Thee may trow the original bottle is bann'd. This is not so. I found the bann'd object. 'Tis located beneath where nature and business converge. Thee must fordo that which ultimately contains the ban. When thou dost, thou shalt break the ban. Thee also shall win the bare treasure."

"Let's start with what we know," Dan said. "Huzza means congratulations. Ban means curse."

"And somehow this is the final riddle," I said. We'd suspected there's be six riddles to go with the six original squares. That did not appear to be the case.

"The most difficult one."

"That makes sense if it's the end of the quest."

"The next sentence, 'Thee may trow the original bottle is bann'd.' What do we think trow means?"

I considered the context. "It might mean 'think'."

"That would make sense. Or maybe 'believe'."

"Yes, I like that better. 'You may believe the original bottle is cursed.'"

"Except then she writes that this belief is wrong and that she found the cursed object."

"Not just that," I said. "She doesn't call it a bottle. It might completely break the pattern we've seen thus far."

"So, it's an unknown object 'located beneath where nature and business converge'. Which square would that be?" Dan asked.

"All the squares celebrate nature, but did any of the squares also have a business connected to them that was at all nature related?"

We combed through our notes on the remaining six original squares— Ellis, Telfair, and Reynolds.

"Ellis Square was known as Market Square for nearly 200 years because of the number of businesses associated with it. That could be a possibility," Dan concluded.

"Telfair Square used to be St James Square, and

named after green space in England, but doesn't appear to have any businesses associated with it. Certainly not in Beatrice's time. I am comfortable removing it as a possibility."

"Sounds good. That leaves Reynolds Square, first known as Lower New Square."

"I might have something," I said, clicking through to another webpage. "Not in Reynolds Square, but there's a historical marker across the street that used to be the site of *Filature*."

"Fila-what?"

"Basically a silk farm. It existed there at the time the square was installed. At least when Beatrice wrote her note."

"That's for sure an intersection of business and nature," Dan said. "What do you think? Ellis or Reynolds."

I pondered the options. "It really could be either. Ellis, with the hundreds of years of a marketplace on a square established for communion with nature, makes sense. But, an actual silk farm producing on the square, while a smaller business overall, also makes sense." I bit my lower lip. "Let's try Reynolds first and cross our fingers."

"Sounds good. What about the rest of the note? 'Thee must fordo that which ultimately contains the ban.' Fordo is the only word throwing me."

"At first, I thought something along the lines of 'find'. But then the next sentence doesn't follow. Just finding the object wouldn't break the curse. We have to do something with the object to break the curse."

"We know it isn't break, since she uses that word separately. Let me check an online thesaurus." He typed on his tablet. "No, no, no, maybe, no. Something like 'separate' or 'bust' or 'destroy'?"

I silently used each of those in the sentence. "I like 'destroy' the best. Beatrice couldn't do it, so she created this counter-curse that builds up the energy, if that makes sense."

"As much as any of this ever does," Dan said with a laugh. "That brings us to the last sentence about winning the treasure. That sounds good, except the word 'bare' is throwing me off."

"What meanings could bare have? Unfortunately, a bare cupboard springs to mind, which means empty. No actual treasure."

"Let me check the thesaurus again." Dan typed. "Other possibilities besides there being no treasure could be 'simple' or 'exposed'."

"With pirates, exposed seems unlikely. If it makes you feel better, we'll go with simple instead of empty." I quirked an eyebrow.

"Thanks, boss. Okay, so, our translated note reads: 'Congratulations! Well done on finding the final riddle. You have almost proven yourselves worthy enough to break the pirate's curse. As it is the final riddle, this one will not be so easy as the others have been. You may believe the original bottle is cursed. This is not so. I found the cursed object. It is located beneath where nature and business converge. You must destroy that which ultimately contains the curse. When you do, you will break the curse. You also will win the simple treasure.'"

I clapped in anticipation. "Looks like we're off to Reynolds Square to find a cursed object and break Basilica's curse."

CHAPTER TWENTY-THREE

"This one will definitely be trickier," I said, as we stood before the *Filature* historical marker across the street from Reynolds Square.

"Sure. Though we know it isn't here, right?" Dan asked, pointing at the spot where we stood.

"Correct." I spun to face the square. "It's somewhere in there. Unfortunately, without knowing the prior setup of the silk production, I think we have to immediately seek assistance from a resident ghost."

"Copy that."

Dan and I crossed the street to enter the square in the last gasps of dusk. Even in the dimming light, it matched the other squares, with stately trees, red brick pathways, and wooden benches. We walked toward the primary monument, a bronze statue of John Wesley, a Methodist missionary. A nearby bench became our new home. Dan pulled out his tablet and began searching for a ghost.

"Hmm," he muttered.

"That doesn't sound good."

"This one might be tricky."

"Trickier than a marble statue of a 6-year-old girl?"

"How about nameless people who died of malaria?"

"Ouch. Touché."

"It gets worse."

"Worse than dying of malaria?"

"According to this website about hauntings in Savannah, the people who died were wrapped in sheets and burned in the square. Right here."

I shuddered.

"When people take pictures of that," he said, pointing to the monument before us, "they report unexplained spots and such in the photos."

"Ghosts, perhaps?"

"Hopefully."

"Here goes." I closed my eyes, visualized my stone protection wall soaring high as my mind could see. With great care, I removed a single stone. It vanished in my mind. Then another one. And another. I sensed energy pulsating on the other side of the wall and fervently hoped it was malaria patients, and not Basilica Hands, waiting to assault my mind again.

When I felt open and ready, I called out to the formless energy. *Is anyone there who can help us?*

Swirling energy of red, orange, and black built up in

my mind. Much more than I expected; much darker too. With each removed stone, the turbulent energy built in my mind. The concentration soared, higher than anything I had encountered previously, yet did not try to enter my mind. It was the strangest thing.

All energy pushed against my wall and took advantage of its removal. I'd honestly thought of the energy like water, that it just flowed in every available crevice. But, perhaps I'd been wrong. For this energy to grow to such an overwhelming and potentially overpowering amount, but not approach me psychically astounded me. Savannah earned its reputation as one of the most haunted cities in the country. I stopped removing protection stones and reached out to the swirling mass.

No response from the energy blob. Except… wait. That wasn't accurate. If I wasn't mistaken, based on the paling and shrinking of the colors, the blob had withdrawn from me in response. That flabbergasted me further.

We need help finding a lost object.

No response from the energy blob at all this time. Maybe I was misunderstanding what the energy mass represented. Could it be something other than ghost energy?

Please, it's a matter of life and death.

That time, a pinprick of energy brightened in my mind. I opened my eyes and spoke into our plane of existence, repeating my plea.

The air shimmered before me. An apparition of a man in a sheet appeared before me. A twenty-something man with a white sheet wrapped around his thin body stared at me. His jaundiced eyes gleamed, maybe with fever, and blue lips housed cold sores.

"Can you help us?" I whispered my question.

He blinked and his mouth opened and closed, but he said nothing.

"Do you understand me?" I tried instead.

The man nodded.

"Can you speak?"

One shoulder rose and fell.

I wasn't sure what that meant, but rolled with the challenge. "There's an object buried somewhere in the square that we need to find."

The man nodded.

"We don't know what it is, except that it presumably isn't large, and it should be giving off negative supernatural energy from a curse."

He grimaced.

"It hasn't hurt any of the others who have helped us." I bit my lower lip. "Do you think it might harm you?" I didn't know how it could be different, but the supernatural realm remained largely a mystery; my clairempathy barely tapped into it.

Another one-shoulder shrug in response.

"Do you think you can help us find it?"

The man stared at me. Just when I despaired that he would refuse, he nodded.

Relief flooded me, and I told Dan that the ghost had agreed. I explained to the malaria victim how the prior ghosts had assisted us. "I'm not sure what energy exactly that they searched for, or could see or sense below the surface." Now I shrugged, but it was more from helplessness. "I know that's not terribly helpful."

The ghost turned from us and started gliding forward. Interesting that he didn't walk as the others had.

I jumped to my feet to follow, with Dan right behind me.

The ghost glided.

We followed.

He crisscrossed the square.

We followed.

He backtracked.

We followed.

Finally, we were back at the bench where we'd started. A frisson of anxiety rolled up and down my spine.

The ghost faced us. He shook his head.

"Nothing?"

He shook his head again.

"Are you sure?"

He nodded his head.

"You didn't sense any objects with emanating energy?"

His lips pursed, possibly in confusion.

"Um, emitting or releasing energy," I tried to clarify. "Anything unusual or not typical of a real object."

He shook his head.

Frustration built. I realized I'd likely reached the limit of the ghost's ability to assist. I nodded at him. "Thank you so much for your help. I understand the object isn't here."

As the ghost faded from our realm, a high-pitched bark of laughter echoed in my mind.

"Did you hear that?" I asked Dan, even though I knew the answer.

"That high-pitched shriek?"

My eyes widened. "You heard that?" The laughter repeated, louder and longer.

His eyes widened to match mine. "There it is again. Faint, though. Based on your reaction, I'm guessing you hear it much louder. Is it the ghost?" His voice tinged with excitement. "Am I hearing a ghost?"

"Somehow, I think so," I said. "That's not good, that he—or the curse—has grown that strong."

"Are you okay?"

"I'm about to not be," I warned him.

YO-HO-HO.

"No," I muttered, snapping my eyes shut and focusing on rebuilding my wall.

TIME TO WALK THE PLANK.

"Get out of my head," I rasped, frantically replacing stone walls. A loud rumble rolled through my mind. The stones were falling! All of them, it seemed, in an avalanche. How was that possible?

Was this Basilica?

Was this more evidence of the curse worsening?

When my phone shrilled an incoming call, I guessed that would be our clients. My hand shook as I passed my cellphone to Dan to answer.

I stayed inwardly focused, though outwardly spread

my legs as if to brace myself for a physical attack. My balled fists hung at my sides.

Get out of my head! I shouted at Basilica in my mind, while I struggled to rebuild my wall of protection. I reversed the flow of the stones from the avalanche, like watching a movie backward. The stones flew back up as fast as they had come down.

DEAD MEN TELL NO TALES.

I grasped the sides of my face, aware of tears streaming down my cheeks. The stones plummeted again and the angry, gleeful energy consumed me. No doubt, I looked delirious. Dan placed his hand on my back and I took comfort in the support. With every ounce of concentration, my mind grabbed ahold of each stone and flung with all its might to replace it.

Get out of my head! I shouted again at Basilica in my mind.

Slowly, oh so slowly, the stones flew back to my wall, as I forced out the ghost's toxic energy.

My eyes flew open with the last stone placement. I twisted to face Dan. "He's gone."

"Thank goodness. Let's sit." Dan guided me to the closest bench, and I collapsed on it. He handed me a tissue to wipe my eyes and nose.

"Thanks. I'm sure you gathered that our ghost with malaria didn't find anything."

"Indeed." Dan frowned.

"What else?"

"It gets worse."

"Worse than the cursed object not being here, you hearing a ghost for the first time, and Basilica wrecking my wall of protection?"

Dan inclined his head in acceptance of my reasoning. And although he no doubt wanted to ask me about the end of my statement, instead he said, "The call was from Christine Mackey. While you were fighting off Basilica, Jimmy had an episode."

"An episode?"

"He started pacing around their rental, yelling about getting to the treasure before anyone else. He kept repeating that he was the only one worthy, and would stop anyone who got in his way."

"Oh no," I exclaimed. "What did Christine do?"

"She pretended to agree with him to keep him in the room. Eventually, he stopped. Maybe when you kicked Basilica out of your mind? She said he immediately fell asleep. She says he looks terrible. Huge bags under his eyes, sallow skin. He somehow looks like he's aged years."

"We're running out of time," I whispered.

"What next?"

"We have to try the other square. The object must be there."

It had to be.

CHAPTER TWENTY-FOUR

In complete desperation, I jogged the third of a mile up Bryan Street from Reynolds Square to Ellis Square. Dan moved slower so that he could review the history of the square. My heart sank when he reached me, standing at the edge of the square, and filled me in.

This square had undergone more transformation than any of the other squares in Savannah. It started as Decker Square, which was what Beatrice would have known it as. Also during her time, the unofficial name was Market Square, which was why we'd considered it a contender for the square where commerce and nature intersected.

The problem was that the square had been razed 200 years later for, of all things, a parking garage. Thankfully, when that lease ran out, public outcry resulted in the city resurrecting the square, renaming it Ellis.

Except the company that had destroyed the original square certainly would have dug deeper than a foot into the ground to prepare for laying the garage concrete. Then the city moved the parking garage underground. Before putting the new square back on top. Unless the object truly had some kind of supernatural protection around it to prevent a disturbance, the chances of a cursed object being here were virtually zero.

Standing in Ellis Square, one would never know all of that history. But you would know it differed from the rest of Savannah's squares. When the city's planners reimagined it, they reimagined it. The square contained both concrete and red brick walkways, tons of open grassy areas, plus the famous dancing fountains. But none of that mattered to me at the moment.

"Any hauntings?" I asked Dan, who scoured the internet on his tablet. We perched on the top step of the low stairs that outlined the square. To prepare for Dan finding a ghost to contact, I removed a single stone from my protection wall. Nausea roiled through me, and I shoved the stone back into the hole. That wasn't good.

"I'm not finding anything," he said.

That wasn't good either. "Not a single haunting?"

"Nothing that's been reported. Doesn't mean it isn't actually haunted," he reminded me.

"True." I wrapped an arm around my stomach, which burbled still from the brief removal of the stone from my protection wall. "It's just easier to contact a ghost with a name."

"Yeah." He kept typing. "The square had been the site for slave auctions; possibly you could reach a ghost who either died here or stayed connected because of the horror of an auction."

Trepidation swelled within me. I hated the thought of stirring up the restless spirit of someone who'd been sold at a slave auction. "Since I don't have a name of anyone specific, I'm going to put the request out there and hope for the best." I offered Dan a trembling smile; his expression told me he wasn't buying my false bravado.

I closed my eyes and began dismantling my wall of protection again, this time bracing myself for the onslaught of physical distress.

And it was a good thing I did.

Horrific emotions of fear, anger, and sadness washed over me.

My stomach clenched, spasming in an effort to vomit.

Pain coiled in my head.

I swallowed against the agony and pleaded with— well, I wasn't certain. There was energy there, for sure. Not like the visible ball from the earlier square. But definite energy.

We need help. I know you do not need to. Probably don't want to. But a family is being torn apart.

No response to my plea, though the pain in my head surged and the anger threatened to drown my mind.

I repeated my entreaty.

Nothing.

And again.

I'm sorry to have intruded. I'm sorry for what they did to you. We'll leave now.

"Wait. I will try."

I opened my eyes in response to the incongruously young-sounding but deep voice. In front of me stood a teenager, brown eyes peering out of a face that had seen too much. He wore a light-colored button-down shirt with the sleeves rolled up and the hem tucked into light-colored pants that stopped at his ankles. He was barefoot.

"I have observed for a long time," the teen continued. "Much has changed in the world. I have changed in my world."

My jaw dropped open. I snapped it shut. "Thank you so much. I'm Sarah. What can I call you?"

"Ellick."

"Thank you, Ellick." I explained to him what we needed.

Much like the ghosts before him, he turned to survey the square, before gesturing that we should follow him.

And so we did.

From corner to corner.

Around the edges.

Retracing steps several times until we were sure.

We finally stopped back at the low stairs where we'd started the search.

"I am sorry," Ellick said.

"Me too," I agreed, the weight of those words carrying much more than I could offer.

"Good luck." At that, Ellick shimmered off our plane.

"You too," I whispered into the empty air.

"Now what?" Dan asked.

I didn't know how to answer him. The cursed object wasn't in either of the squares that seemed to be a reasonable fit for Beatrice's final riddle.

We'd failed.

No. I refused to accept that. Not when lives were in danger.

I slumped on the top step. Dan sat beside me.

"Let's talk through the last riddle. We must have missed something," I said.

"Like what? Isn't it possible the object is just long gone?"

I shook my head. "It is. But, since this square wasn't as strong of a contender as Reynolds Square was, it occurred to me that maybe Reynolds wasn't that strong either." My brain calculated, chasing the idea that had bubbled to the surface.

"What do you mean?"

"Beatrice said the cursed object isn't another rum bottle. What if the final location isn't a Savannah square?"

CHAPTER TWENTY-FIVE

Dan gaped at me. "What do you mean, the final location isn't a Savannah square? What am I missing?"

"We started with the assumption that there would be six riddles to correspond with the six original squares."

"Yes."

"We were wrong."

"Yes."

"Then because the first riddles brought us to rum bottles, we assumed that all of them would be rum bottles."

Dan nodded. "And we assumed that because the first riddles brought us to squares, that all the riddles would bring us to squares."

I pointed at him. "Exactly. Since we were wrong about the rum bottle for this final riddle, why can't we also be wrong about the final location?"

"We've been wrong before," Dan said, then frowned. "Where do we think the final object is?"

"That, I have no idea. We need to look at the exact wording of the riddle again."

Dan pulled the translation up on his tablet and tilted it so I could see it in the early evening darkness. I reread it silently first.

'Congratulations! Well done on finding the final riddle. You have almost proven yourselves worthy enough to break the pirate's curse. As it is the final riddle, this one will not be so easy as the others have been. You may believe the original bottle is cursed. This is not so. I found the cursed object. It is located beneath where nature and business converge. You must destroy that which ultimately contains the curse. When you do, you will break the curse. You also will win the simple treasure.'

"The key is the line about nature and business converging. If we remove the possibility of it being an official square, what does that leave us?" I scratched at my chin absentmindedly.

"Beatrice wouldn't have stashed a haunted object just anywhere. It has to have meaning for her."

"I agree. What would be a location that would have meaning for her in 1755, as the daughter of a pirate in Savannah?"

Neither of us spoke as we typed on our devices, trying to find a reasonable solution. I discarded the options that my searches suggested. Until I simplified my approach and searched the internet for '1755 pirate secret Savannah'.

"Oh wow," I exclaimed. "I might have something."

"Do tell."

"Have you heard of The Pirate's House?"

"Sound familiar. Did it come up earlier today? Give me more."

"It's one of the oldest buildings in the entire state. It's currently a restaurant in Savannah, on the river." I scanned the open webpage. "But it operated as an inn when it opened in 1753."

"That fits our timeline."

"It gets even better. The inn was a meeting spot of sorts for pirates. It became quite well known for that. And the building is basically next door to the Knight House."

"Those are good connections to our pirate daughter."

I smiled. "There's more."

"Ooh, you found something juicy."

"I did. There were secret tunnels underneath the inn. Pirates used them to kidnap people. They'd get drunk, pass out, and then wake up on a ship, in servitude to a pirate."

Dan's eyes widened. "That sounds like the perfect place to stash a haunted object."

"Indeed." I typed more, searching for the last piece of the puzzle. And I found it. "There used to be a tunnel off the rum cellar. Reportedly, it's since been boarded up, but it ran the block from there to the sea."

"The easier for moving kidnapped men, I suppose?"

"Yep." I closed the tab and placed my cellphone in my jeans pocket. "And the perfect place to hide a haunted object that's tied to piracy. Consider Beatrice's childhood and the line in her note about the object 'located beneath where nature and business converge'."

"Beneath makes sense for a tunnel. Business makes sense for both the inn and for kidnapping people to work for you, I suppose. Where does 'nature' come in?"

"This might be a stretch," I admitted, "but I wonder if Beatrice was being more figurative here. Maybe she was talking about the nature of man, more generally, as opposed to actual nature?"

"What do you mean?"

"The rumor was that pirates kidnapped drunk men. Perhaps she was referring to the nature of man?"

Dan nodded slowly. "I could see that."

"It's the best lead we have now."

"It's the only one we have right now. Is the tunnel still there?"

"I sure hope so, or we're in trouble."

CHAPTER TWENTY-SIX

Dan and I stood in front of The Pirate's House. In the dark, we couldn't see the details, but we learned a lot from scanning pictures online. The multi-storied house had gray wood mixed with exposed brick. Light blue shutters framed the handful of windows. We entered the busy restaurant, amid their dinner rush. Tourists, I figured. Like us. A hostess approached and asked if we had a reservation.

"We don't," I said. Before she could respond, I pitched my voice low and continued. "Is there a manager available? It's rather important."

The young lady opened her mouth, perhaps to ask what we needed, and maybe decided it was above her pay grade. "I'll get the manager. Please wait here."

I thanked her and then waited with Dan, checking out the interior. Lots of dark wood everywhere. The tables. The flooring. The ceiling. At least during the day, there were windows to let in plenty of light.

Plus, the sounds of happiness and laughter. People were definitely having a good time here. I considered removing a stone from my wall of protection to enjoy the happiness more, but thought better of the impulse. If the building was haunted, that could be a disaster in the making.

"Hello, I'm Matthew Williams." An early thirty-something man stood before me, arm extended. "I'm the manager of The Pirate House. How can I help you?"

I accepted the outstretched hand and stepped closer, deciding at that moment on a limited version of the truth. "I'm Doctor Sarah Danger, and I have a favor to ask."

"Doctor Danger? Really?"

"I can show you my driver's license," I assured him. My phone chose that inopportune time to ring, so I silenced it without checking the number.

"What can I do for you, Doctor Danger?"

I briefly explained my background as a supernatural investigator, informed him about the pirate's curse, and asked to inspect the rum cellar rumored to house the tunnel to the sea. It was fun watching his expression change from open to confused to incredulous.

"Ma'am, even if I wanted to—" His expression expressed that he did not. "—that area of the restaurant is off-limits to visitors outside of tour groups. It's the oldest section of the building, and we do not allow unaccompanied tourists, for liability reasons."

"If you're with us, we wouldn't be unaccompanied then, would we?"

He frowned.

Leaning even closer, I whispered, "And if there's a haunted object in that tunnel? Are you prepared to handle an angry pirate ghost if he sets his sights on you?"

Mr. Williams appeared less certain.

Dan's phone rang, and he mimicked my action, silencing it without checking the number.

"What's the harm?" I asked the manager, opening my arms, elbows at my waist. "What if the alternative is people die?" Manipulative, sure, but lives were at stake. Unfortunately, it didn't work.

"Ma'am, it isn't happening. I'm going to need you and your colleague to leave." He spun to walk way.

I reached out a hand to touch his elbow.

He spun back around, as if preparing for a fight.

I held up my hands up in supplication. "Relax. I'm not going to attack you." I dropped one hand and indicated Dan with the other. "It sounds crazy, I know, but we really do solve supernatural mysteries. And people really will die if we fail."

The manager's expression of disdain wavered.

"Surely you've heard of my blog," Dan jumped in with an incongruous wink. "It's called *A Doctor Danger Mystery* and it's about Sarah here working as a Supernatural Specialist. It's gotten quite a bit of attention."

Mr. Williams snapped his fingers and grinned. "That's why your name, albeit ridiculous, sounded familiar. My wife loves your blog. She checks in nearly every day to see if there's a new entry."

"See, we're legit," Dan said.

I could have kissed him in that moment. My cheeks flushed at the thought, but luckily nobody else noticed.

"We can go down to the cellar," the manager now agreed. "My wife would never forgive me for not helping. But we have to go fast. Follow me." He spun on his heels and strode away from us. Dan and I scrambled to follow.

We maneuvered through the building to an older area with lower ceilings. We passed a cool clock made of a dark metal before arriving at a sign reading, in part,

'According to legend… This stairway at one time led to the entrance of a tunnel which ran from the old rum cellar beneath The Pirates' House to the banks of the Savannah River… a short block away.'

Dan and I stared down the dark stairs next to the sign. The stairs curved to the left and reached a brick basement.

The manager stepped down the stairs, and we followed silently. My clumsiness chose that moment to assert itself, and I tripped. An arm grabbed me from behind, keeping me from knocking the manager over like a bowling pin. Dan steadied me with one hand, while his other snaked around my middle until I caught my breath.

"That was close," I said, heat suffusing my face. "Good thing you were there."

Before Dan could respond, the manager called up. "Please don't hurt yourselves. I'm already asking for trouble here."

"We're coming," I called down, disentangling myself from Dan's arms. I sensed him remain close as we continued down and joined Mr. Williams at the bottom of the staircase.

We found ourselves in a room that time forgot. The low wooden ceiling had matching wooden crossbeams, all faded to gray. A similar dusty gray wood covered the floors. The walls were red brick with many spots that had worn or crumbled away. The room was clearly old, but on one end of it sat a fake treasure chest, opened to reveal the pirate's booty. I stifled a chuckle at that visual, but figured the tourists loved it. Next to the chest was a similar wall, but with a crude tunnel-sized hole cut in it, with black metal sconces on either side.

"Here we are." The manager stood to the side, watching us take in the room. "Do what you need to do. But, hurry, there's a tour group due soon."

"Of course there is," I mumbled, but there was no need to hurry. As soon as we'd entered the space, energy pressed in on me. So far, it felt neutral, but that could change in an instant. The space had strong residual energy. Whether from kidnapping people or just smuggling illegal alcohol during prohibition, I couldn't tell.

"Dan, I'm going to open myself up. Be ready."

"Got it, boss."

"Be ready for what?" the manager asked, a note of worry tinging his question.

I stood in the center of the room. Closing my eyes, I removed a single stone from my wall of protection. A single burst of energy buffeted me. I removed a second stone and sent out my silent request for assistance. I'd considered asking Dan to search for a specific ghost, but I sensed that wouldn't be necessary here because—

"What are ye doing?"

The voice bellowed, and my eyes popped open. Basilica Hands stood in front of the fake tunnel entrance.

"Be gone, ye filthy dog o' 'ere!" The ghost shrieked.

"Did someone say something?" Dan asked, his tone cautious.

"You heard him again?" I responded, aghast.

"Heard who?" Mr. Williams interrupted, though we didn't answer.

"Basilica definitely doesn't want us here." At my statement, Basilica flew toward me. I flinched backward.

"Be gone!" he repeated, and I imagined spectral spit hitting my face.

"Be ready," I murmured to Dan.

He nodded.

"I'm looking for your daughter's cursed object," I said, choosing my words carefully.

Basilica looked uncertain. "Beatrice?"

"Yes, Basilica, I'm searching for the object that Beatrice cursed."

"Why would Beatrice curse anything?" The pirate ghost sounded genuinely confused.

"She placed a counter-curse to end your curse."

His expression hardened. "She would not betray family."

"Basilica, she did it because of family."

"That makes no sense."

"Think about it," I said, aware that I looked like a lunatic to the restaurant manager, talking to the air. "Beatrice loved you very much. You were her father. When her mother—"

"Eleanor." The pirate's voice softened the most I'd heard it.

"Yes, Eleanor. When she died, Beatrice found your original cursed rum bottle."

"Only the worthy shall inherit the treasure." Basilica tried for bombastic, but it was clear his confusion was growing.

"Exactly. Beatrice remembered your ravings about a curse when you were dying of yellow fever. Do you remember that?"

Basilica didn't respond, but he was closely following my words.

"She was a child then and didn't think it was real. When she found the bottle, she took it to a hoodoo practitioner. Unfortunately, you did too good of a job, Basilica. The practitioner couldn't break the curse. Beatrice needed an alternative."

"Beatrice always was a quick child," Basilica said, with something that sounded an awful lot like admiration mixed with fatherly love.

"With the practitioner's help, Beatrice identified another object, placed a counter-curse, and then hid a series of riddles around the city. The only way to remove your curse was to solve her riddles and destroy the object on which she placed the counter-curse."

Basilica's skin had taken on a greenish tone.

"Are you okay?" I asked.

"I… don't know."

"Can you help us? Do you know where the cursed object is in here? We believe Beatrice hid it in the underground tunnel, because of its connection to piracy at that time."

Basilica grimaced. "No."

"No? No, you can't help us or no, you don't know where the object is." Now I was the confused one.

"It's too late." The pirate ghost's voice was forlorn with the pronouncement that coincided with loud voices and objects crashing above us.

Our heads swiveled up as if we could see through the ceiling above. More crashing sounds. More shouting.

"That does not sound good," Dan said.

"No, it does not," I agreed.

The manager had rushed to the base of the stairway, but he didn't step up. His face became ashen.

Feet clomped as someone descended the stairs.

The manager stepped backward.

James Mackey Junior entered the room clumsily, barely avoiding falling. His bloodshot eyes scanned us before his cracked lips parted and he yelled, "The treasure is mine. I'm the worthy one."

"Jimmy!" I exclaimed.

"How did he get here?" Dan asked.

"Who is this?" Mr. Williams asked in bewilderment.

Jimmy took a few strangled breaths before staggering into the room. He appeared disoriented.

"Is he drunk?" Dan whispered.

"Jimmy, are you okay?" I asked, already noticing I was feeling unsteady on my feet.

Jimmy focused on me. "You can't stop me."

"I know that," I hollered back, hands on my hips. "Why would I? We can get the treasure together."

My outburst threw Jimmy.

"What is wrong with you?" I continued, angry confusion sweeping through me. "Help me get the pirate to tell us where the treasure is. We've almost got it." Sweat poured off my brow. I lifted a hand to wipe it away before it could blur my vision. Had someone turned the heat up?

Basilica stepped between me and Jimmy. "Neither of you is worthy. You're both going to die."

"No," I said with deadly calm.

Jimmy didn't speak, but instead threw himself at me.

He didn't reach me. Dan jumped between us, tackling the teenager. They crashed to the floor. The violence of it shook Jimmy's hold over my emotions.

"Thank you," I whispered to Dan, leaning over, hands on my knees, trying to catch my breath and clear my head. I couldn't risk rebuilding my wall of protection while I communicated with Basilica. I needed either him or another ghost to find the cursed object in the real tunnel from this room.

Without Basilica's help, I didn't know what we'd do.

CHAPTER TWENTY-SEVEN

Jimmy had knocked himself out cold when he hit the floor. That was what released his hold over me. Dan sat beside Jimmy on the ground, cradling his head. Basilica, on the other hand, seemed to be fading. I couldn't let him do that. We needed him to help find his daughter's counter-cursed object, whatever it was, wherever it was. I sensed the energy, so I believed it was here. Somewhere.

"Basilica," I whispered to the ghost. He stood about ten feet from me, legs hip-distance apart, arms dangling at his sides. He appeared to be sleeping standing up, his head hung down, eyes closed. At my use of his name, his head rose.

"What?" The single word, devoid of any inflection.

"We need your help. Your daughter didn't want you to do this."

"Beatrice."

"Yes, Beatrice." I struggled to form the right words. His apathy was draining me. "Do you remember getting sick? Before you… died."

The pirate nodded, his lank locks falling over his face. He didn't brush them off.

"While you were sick, did you think about Blackbeard's treasure?"

"Argh. He shot me."

The non sequitur threw me. "What?"

"I remember." Basilica's eyes seemed clearer than they had since I'd met him. "Blackbeard shot me to remind everyone he was in charge and could do whatever he wanted. When he died and everyone was—" I swore he audibly swallowed here. "—tried and hung, I was it. The one who knew where the treasure was. I'd earned it. It was mine."

"Of course you did," I said, using my soothing voice for us both. I'd felt the prick of righteous irritation rise in me at his statement.

"I told ever'one I was going to England. But I didn't. Instead, I became the illegitimate son of Thomas Knight after he died." The pirate laughed, a harsh phlegmy sound. "Knight turned on us, so I turned on him. Then, became him." He offered a toothy grin, which I mirrored, before catching myself.

"I used the treasure. Slowly, carefully. Bought the house. Took care of me wife and daughter." He frowned. "Then I started coughing. An seeing things. Believed people would take me treasure. I needed to protect it." This last was said with conviction, the apathy gone.

"You did what you knew to do."

"Blackbeard had shown me about the hoodoo. I knew where to go. Paid the last of me treasure to do it."

He sounded so proud, yet he missed the importance of what he'd said.

"If the treasure was gone, why did you curse the bottle?" I asked.

"There's no treasure?" Dan asked from the floor.

I ignored Dan and repeated my question to Basilica. "If the treasure was gone, why did you curse the bottle?"

"I…" his voice trailed off. "I don't know."

"You were sick. Dying. You didn't know what you were doing," I filled in for him. "And if we don't find the object Beatrice hid, that young man right there," I said, pointing at Jimmy, who was waking up, "his family, and even me, we will die."

"It matters not. Ever'body dies."

"Yes, Basilica, they do," I agreed. "But this young man, Jimmy. He's the son of James and Christine. Like Beatrice was your's and Elizabeth's daughter. How would you have felt if someone took Beatrice from you?"

Basilica appeared stricken. "No, 'tis not right."

"It's going to happen," I insisted. "Unless you help us find and destroy the object Beatrice hid."

"How?"

I explained how previous ghosts had helped us find the bottles Beatrice had hidden containing the riddles. Basilica agreed to try, and in a weird déjà vu moment, began crisscrossing the small space, sensing for the exact location of his daughter's counter-cursed object. He stopped in front of the tunnel-size false opening in the wall.

"That's not a real tunnel," I objected.

"The best things hide in plain sight," the manager quipped, and we all stared at him.

"That's the entrance to the secret tunnels?" I asked, dumbfounded.

He shrugged.

"Can we enter it?" Dan asked.

"Normally, I'd say no, but this seems unusual enough to grant an exception," Mr. Williams said. He brushed his hands down the sides of his pant legs as if knocking off dust. "Let me call for help." He pulled his cellphone out of his pocket and texted someone. There ensued a few back-and-forth communications.

"I want to help," a soft voice came from our feet.

"We'll let you know if we need you, Jimmy. I promise," I assured the teenager, who smiled wanly.

Footsteps on the stairs drew our attention. The hostess from before stepped down, a puzzled expression on her face. She ignored us and brought a sledgehammer to the manager. "Are you sure?"

"Just stay upstairs, no matter what you hear," he instructed her.

After she left, he flashed a smile. "To be honest, I've always wanted to do this." He swung the sledgehammer up and over his shoulder before bringing it down in the center of the tunnel-sized outline. Several swings later, the dust settled, and our group stared into what was clearly a brick tunnel.

"I want to go, too," Jimmy said from the floor, his voice sounding stronger.

"Jimmy, are you… okay… to do this?" I asked the teenager, who had staggered to his feet with Dan's help.

"I think so," he said. "Banging my head on the floor brought me to my senses." He offered a lop-sided grin.

My guess was Basilica's emotional softening was the source of Jimmy feeling better, but we had somewhere to be.

I led the way, stepping over the pile of bricks into the tunnel. It had an arched roof and the entire thing was constructed of discolored red brick. The safety was questionable, given the age and disrepair, but a wave of energy rolled over me, confirming we were on the right path.

"Was that a shot across the bow?" Basilica asked, hand reaching for his sheathed knife.

"Was that a warning shot?" I translated. The others stared at me in confusion. "You felt the energy too?"

Basilica nodded.

I sneezed from the dust hanging in the air. Clearing my throat, I pointed forward. "Let's find our counter-cursed object."

Our motley crew crept through the tunnel, the light from my cellphone in front, and the light from the cellar at our backs.

I didn't think Beatrice would have gone far back then. Nor did I believe she would use something of value for her object. I was right on one count, but not the other.

I halted at the same moment Basilica shouted in my ear, "Heave!"

Aiming the cellphone flashlight in a circle around us, I watched for something to be out of place, since the tunnel appeared empty.

And there it was. A single brick, sticking out enough from the others that you'd find it if you knew what you were looking for, but otherwise would remain invisible against the rest of the bricks. I held my phone in my left hand, angling the light at the brick while I used my right hand to ever so gently wiggle the brick free of the wall. That it slid out relatively easily confirmed my suspicion. I set the brick on the floor and shone my light into the cavity revealed.

Light reflected at me. I reached my hand into the crevice and withdrew a tarnished locket.

"What is that?" Dan asked.

"Shiver me timbers! Beatrice," Basilica said, his voice thick with emotion.

"Was this your daughter's?"

He nodded.

I used my fingernails to open the heart-shaped locket, inscribed with the initials BH on the front. Beatrice Hands. Although she would have been Beatrice Knight. Could it represent Basilica Hands? The locket popped open. I gasped, nearly dropping the golden treasure.

Inside wasn't a picture or set of pictures, but a lock of hair.

"Is that your hair, Basilica?" I asked the ghost.

"'Tis."

"I think we can not only break the curse, but set you free," I said to him.

Basilica remained silent, but his posture straightened and a wave of hope poured off him.

"Would you like us to try?"

A curt nod was the response.

I supposed that was the best I could do. The amount of emotional turmoil Basilica had experienced, and was experiencing, was probably overwhelming him. "Does anyone have a match or a lighter?"

Mr. Williams reached into his pocket. "Been trying to quit." He withdrew a blue lighter, which I accepted.

"Is everybody ready? I don't know what will happen." Solemn nods came from the group. I shook Basilica's lock of hair into my palm and handed the locket to Dan, not missing the way Basilica's eyes followed it. I kneeled to the ground, placing the lock of hair atop the brick I'd removed from the wall. "Be prepared to help me put this out if it spreads," I joked.

Nobody laughed.

I thumbed at the back of the lighter. It took a few tries, and then a shimmer of light sparked. I held it to the lock of hair and it caught. The hair burned bright and fast, the scent of sulfur filling the enclosed space. Covered coughs sounded as we watched the hair burn itself out.

The staggering amount of energy dissipated with the hair. I jumped to my feet to face Basilica, expecting him to fade with the energy. Instead, a soft light formed around him as his eyes cleared of their madness and he beamed at me.

No, not at me. At someone behind me.

I turned and gasped. Two women stood, hand-in-hand. Their similar masses of brown curls, facial structure, and 18th-century clothing told me who they were before Basilica spoke their names.

"Ellie. Beatrice. 'Tis really you?" Basilica's voice, though now sane and hearty, sounded uncertain. "You look older."

"This is the age we were when we died." The woman on the right faced me. "I'm Beatrice."

"Beatrice," I exclaimed, ignoring the gasps from the others who couldn't see our ghostly visitors. "You must be Eleanor, then," I addressed the woman on the left, who offered a courtesy and shy smile.

Basilica crossed past me to join his family. He smelled pleasantly musky, instead of like mold and decay. His wife and daughter embraced him for a long moment.

Tears slid down my cheeks and warmth flowed through me at the beauty of the otherworldly family reunion.

Basilica, flanked on either side by Eleanor and Beatrice, nodded his thanks at me.

"Thank you for solving my riddles. I hoped it would save someone from a horrible death, but," she paused to look at her father, "I never imagined I would get my father back, too."

"You're all welcome," I said, sniffling. "Thank you, Beatrice, for creating the trail for us to follow. Without you, none of this would have been possible."

The reunited family gazed at each other as they faded from view.

I sniffled again and wiped a tear from my eye.

"You'll have to tell me what happened just then," Dan whispered.

"We did it. The curse is broken."

CHAPTER TWENTY-EIGHT

The Mackeys had gone all out, creating the brunch feast before us. All four of them had a glow of health that had been sorely lacking when I'd met them only yesterday. The impact of the ghost's curse had truly been killing them.

Us. I felt better than I had since I met them, too.

"Thank you, Sarah and Dan, for everything you did to bring Jimmy home and to end this nightmare," Christine said, lifting her glass of orange juice in a toast.

Everyone at the table lifted a glass of juice, milk, or water.

"You're welcome. I'm just glad we were able to do so," I demurred, glancing at Dan sitting across from me.

James spoke from the head of the table opposite Christine. "When Jimmy broke the window to escape…" His jaw clenched. "I'd never been so frightened in my life."

Beside me, Kelsey chimed in, "I heard the window breaking."

"You were invaluable, honey," her mother assured her and the teen beamed.

"Saved the day," Jimmy teased, and he frowned across at her when she kicked him under the table.

"This one was tricky," I conceded. "You'll get the full report along with my invoice."

"Worth every penny," Christine said.

"Tell your friends," Dan said out of the corner of his mouth.

"Always my biggest supporter," I said, and we shared a look. Working together, finding ourselves in danger, he'd always been there for me. Dan was truly my best friend. Who would have thought? "This will make a great story for the blog," I told him.

The teens perked up at the idea of becoming internet famous, but the parents looked less thrilled.

"Don't worry, we use fake names," I assured Christine and James.

The kids deflated as the parents appeared relieved.

I smothered a laugh. "This afternoon we head back to Tampa and our everyday lives."

"Until the next case, anyway." Dan lifted his glass at me.

"Until next time," I agreed, sipping my drink, enjoying the taste and sensation, savoring both the sweet juice and our sweeter win.

AUTHOR'S NOTE

A great deal of research happened to ground this story in Savannah's rich history. I traveled to Savannah to get a feel for the energy of the city, as well as visited most, if not all, of their historical landmarks, including walking all of Savannah's Squares. The museums there were also incredibly helpful.

I made tremendous use of the internet, and specifically would like to thank the Georgia Historical Society for their website and email support. I also want to thank LingoJam's Early Modern to Modern English translator and their Pirate Speak translator. These were a great start with creating the linguistic mood.

The history presented in the novel is as accurate as I could make it for the real people and locations, and as realistic as possible for the fictional people and locations. Some, like Basilica, were a mixture of real and fictional, as his history does indeed say he died a penniless beggar in England. Personally, I like my ending for him better!

Huge thank you to everyone in Savannah—including online—who helped me bring the city to life. Any errors made are mine alone, or were details changed for the story.

I hope you enjoyed coming along on Sarah's adventure, and that you, too, can enjoy the wonders of Savannah in your travels.

THANK YOU!

Thank you so much for supporting my work and reading this novel.

If you liked the book, please consider leaving a review online.

Just a few lines would be great. Reviews are not only the highest compliment you can pay to an author, they also help other readers discover and make more informed choices about purchasing books in a crowded online space. Thank you so much in advance.

If you didn't like the book or have concerns, please email me directly at
heather@heathersilvio.com

ABOUT THE AUTHOR

Heather Silvio loves to tell stories, especially fun, flirty, fantasy romance & mystery. She is also an actress and licensed psychologist with a few nonfiction titles for variety. When she isn't working, she channels her inner flapper as a 1920s jazz and blues singer.

Visit https://www.heathersilvio.com for more information and to sign up for her Theatrical Thursdays Newsletter.

www.ingramcontent.com/pod-product-compliance
Lightning Source LLC
Chambersburg PA
CBHW061924220726
48287CB00018B/846